Upstate Pizza Guy in India and Nepal

Notes from a Drifting Road

by Freddie Hoose

Contents

1. Covering Ground

To assess a person's character, ask, "What type of pizza driver would they be?"

And what type of driver am I? I drive in everything—I've got snow tires. Though it wasn't easy at first. You underestimate how far out Hosbach Trail you're going. You've got no house number and some kids from Hamilton High are out there with the stereo so loud they can't hear the phone. Or you take the wrong Hill Road and now you need to go twice the distance in half the time.

I make the delivery so I can make the next delivery, because that one might be the nine-dollar tip. You get an Earlville order half an hour before close. Earlier in the night you jumped at the chance to stay late and sweep up because you need all the cash you can get, plus the other guy's got a kid at home and another job, so it's down Route 12B, past the farm with the concrete cow, to where snow has drifted over the road and the undertow of the wind off the ridges wants to drift you. You and the oncoming truck will meet at the apex of the curve. This could be interesting.

You hang in there for the surprises. The twenty-dollar tip on a church order. The fifteen-dollar tip from the steelworker in the snowstorm. Iroquois dude with a brand new Jeep. Building a library at the college on the hill.

1

I see Madison County at its leisure. Linoleum and the smell of dog, the backyard bonfire in the snow, mom taking up a collection from the family. The trailer down in the hole with kerosene lamps, and when something runs out from under the kitchen table, your brain says *Is that a pig?*

A house number spray-painted on a sheet of plywood and wedged in a snowbank improves my moneymaking ability. Thank you in advance. Guy out in Smyrna loves his chicken parm almost as much as his arsenal. He's twenty minutes out: Take West Rock Road, bomb down through Pharsalia, over the tracks, up Larkin, across Route 80, then straight, straight all the way down the road that borders the State Land and welcomes the characters who want their camps backed up against permaforest. The turkey hunting woods. The guys who plan to save everyone's ass when China invades. He spray-painted *Blend In or Go Hungry* in green and brown on the side of his house.

Get to his place, hop out, knock on the screen door—I used to turn the car around, face it down the driveway and leave it running, but not anymore—knock on the screen door, and then you hear this Frankenstein voice, "Ah, come on in!" But what about the sign: *NO BOOTS IN HOUSE!?*

And he says, "Ah, what's it gonna be!" Artilleryman? As he counts it out, the safe bet is to keep your eyes on the kitchen island with the two long shotguns (so long you have to say it *law-hung*), and don't peek at his daughter on the couch in her military tank-top, don't look at the forty or fifty weapons racked on the walls. A second later, grab your due and the dollar tip and say thanks and bust. He also deals hydro, but not if you're buying retail.

Me, I cultivate tippers. You don't have to be their shrink or their sheep, but you have to play the part. Be their ideal delivery, especially if they don't even realize they have an ideal.

How? Slot the customer into an archetype. Nothing hateful. A freshman guy in the dry dorm with someone in his bed, all teeth? Nerds in love. Apply the Nerds in Love approach. The schema. Formula. Recipe.

2

Style. Yes, style. Because however much you change the approach, it's always a variation on your style. Like driving—smooth shifts are a point of pride.

Do you get drunk when you're snowed in? And then do you call for delivery? If so, we've already met.

I roll exclusively with James Brown. Star Time Disc Four doesn't leave my stereo for six weeks at a time. Keep it on loop, seven times in a night like James would promise. I've analyzed those grooves down to the last fidget. Grooves stripped down to a chapbook, never over. Eminently stackable like broccoli crowns. I bump JB whenever someone might hear it. I want people to turn and ask, "Is that *Funky President?*" and then point to the car stopped at the light with steam pouring from the moonroof. And I want to be seen at that car's wheel.

The Wheelman. The courier, trafficker, smuggler, mule: tied to every delivery all the way back. The Silk Road, Andorra, roughest Afghanistan. I have a bond to UPS, FedEx, DHL. And when I witness a beat-up Neon with a magnetic roof light whip into the Domino's lot way too fast for a place that's a Friday Night Treat for grade schoolers, I say *Yeah, that's how you do it.*

Delhi: The bus is bound for Agra. I sit with my backpack on my lap to avoid paying for a seat to hold its bulk. The sign painted on the concrete wall along the highway says *Mindblowing English Academy*. The next morning, I nap flat on my back on the marble pedestal of the Taj Mahal. The stone does not feel hard. At all.

Two days ago, on my first morning in India, I vomited into a pair of TSA-approved Ziploc bags and dropped them from the window of a city bus. On my first afternoon, I dropped my sunglasses into a squat toilet at the Qutb Minar.

Today I hire a car from Jhansi to Khajuraho, 6 a.m., and doze in the backseat. Is the driver also on the verge of sleep? I may have arranged my own fate to get on the road early. But we live. Culture shock is a form of panic. You don't realize it's happening until it passes.

A man tours the temple in business casual. How much money would I need to move to India and retire? To live on lentils and never work again?

A sickness arrives in the Jaipur railway station. The train is four hours late, and I'm lucky. The first squat comes at midnight. Three more in the next thirty minutes. Then only liquid and looseness until two-thirty when I puke, straight out at eye level.

The train arrives at four, the motions slow down. I ration my bottle of water. Lie parallel to the rails on a bench, and every change of speed jostles my insides toward an exit. At six, I push a man aside as the train pulls out of a farm field's station. Spew four pulls straight down to the tracks, leaning out on the door bars as the train accelerates in the dusky dawn.

At ten, I cough a loogie into the chamber of my throat and lurch to spit it in the bathroom, near my seat at the end of the car. Lower my head toward the western-style bowl, caked with spice. Try to ignore it and hock, but my stomach sends a message. With splashback imminent, I grab a plastic shopping bag from my cargo pocket and push to the space between the cars. Five long pulls fill the bag, cramping and kinking enough to worry about a hernia. Cap it off with dry spasms that wrench up betel nuts from yesterday's paan. But that's it. I'm done.

In Jodhpur I stay plugged for the taxi ride through the old city. Stay loose through the afternoon. The hotel manager brings Electral, the W.H.O. approved formula for cholera. He also brings a vial of aloe pills. The next morning, I eat four pieces of dry toast and two bananas. I wonder why the bread takes thirty minutes to toast. That's how I know I'm hungry again. How I know I'm getting better.

Here it's easy to see how a person can break. Physically—I see my leg broken at a right angle between the ankle and the knee. The roads are ready to break me. The TV commercials have words I don't understand, but the pictures make the point—a hut with a skull and crossbones-shaped cloud of mosquitoes flying in the window. All of entropy's options are on view on the side of the road.

Jodhpur is pushed against the cliff wall under the fort, which makes my heart break for Granada.

People travel light, with only the shawl wrapped around their shoulders, or heavy: burlap sacks, metal steamer trunks, motorcycles wrapped and padded, parcels sealed with wax, feasts in tins, water jugs, or en masse, twelve from the family flooding the rail car.

The crowds support enterprises. The man who makes sandwiches on the station platform has six boys selling, and each boy takes a tray of ten sandwiches to the waiting train. This home of the gypsies, the well of flamenco.

The moneymaking ideas come in a fury. A t-shirt, *Burn Your Guidebook*. A one-page guidebook. A ten-page guidebook. Something map-based. Ten-page sections of guidance, buy what you need. Region by region. Take hiking maps out of the woods and into the cities.

What happened to the last year of my life? The strange comfort of Walmart. Equally frustrating and confusing, the parking lot, too full, too vicious, and on a hill. Park and play cart-ding Russian Roulette. But for someone broke enough to live in a barn in a room with three walls, stocking up can be the highlight of the week.

Fall in upstate New York is regal. You have the roads and the deer and the city by Amtrak. Where to live next? Always the question. Somewhere you can spend a weekend walking if you want.

The postcard hawker sitting on the curb waits all day for the return of the man who said maybe.

The salesman in the street, perfecting the hard sell. *You see, hello! You like? Stop by this* (stop, buy this?), *only 20, 30 dollars. You remember my shop, Number 67.* The newspaper adverts haven't moved past clichés: at your fingertips, make your dreams come true. A land in the infancy of branding.

On the bus, a man sells with the gift-first approach. Foot in the door. *You take this crystal—* And on top of all of the commerce, or below it, a sludge of begging. *Where you from?* An unsolicited guide points out history, where to click the camera. Others sell the price, not the benefit. But this is what we get, what we deserve. *Go where the money is.* Even if no tourist ever bought a thing, the sellers would be here. And they'd be right to be here—the cost of transportation to the subcontinent alone guarantees accessible funds.

Step out of the managed-for-tourism dome and plunge in. Thirty seconds after I board, the bus bombs downhill around the curve. A familiar strategy.

Climb aboard to a standing spot at the top of the stairs, cram amongst a family, a floor loaded with parcels, four kids, two moms, two dads, two aunts... A mom milking on the front seat under her sari, an aunt beside her, holding an orange scarf to the window to shield the sun, a brother beside her with a sister on the knee. Across the aisle, backed up to the driver's cabin and facing the dozens of people packed to the tailgate: Two dads closest to the window, closest to the oncoming traffic, then another aunt, and a tiny head popping from between two pairs of, yes, Indian style laps and starting to squirm, then another mom with another child on her lap, the baby mostly eyes.

At the first stop, I fight to step off and allow people to leave the bus, and fight again to board, and the momentum of new passengers carries me to the almost-back of the bus. I stand in the aisle, pack on the ground. It's too fat for the luggage shelf. Shamefully. In 45 minutes, a seat over the wheels opens up and I grab it. The bus continues on, with my bag lodged between my legs, with me lodged in the seat, through another two kill-the-engine stops, and into Aurangabad (mostly in the path of oncoming traffic) under a sun so low you could pocket it.

And everybody's rocking big Freddie Mercury moustaches. And you can go barefoot anywhere. All the things that could be true are true in India. But tonight, the restaurant is dysfunctional: bread after the meal, drinks staggered by ten minutes, silverware half grimy, half forgotten. The waiter asks me to move tables so the Aurangabad mafia, party of 12, can rule the back two tables over a bottle of Blender's Pride and a bottle of Smirnoff.

An Australian couple across the room. Why not me? They have a Lonely Planet guidebook when they're not. Striped shirts, bought-on-the-beach clothing, with a Nikon worth who knows how many times the average monthly income. The odd piercing. With hotel rooms this cheap, it's even more painful. I could be hosting!

Does everyone do this as a lifestyle? Is everyone at as temporary a stage?

In Delhi, they are carving a temple with lasers. In one day, I sprinted to the Qutb Minar, the Lotus Temple, the Akshardham temple, and then dinner at Karim's next to Asia's largest mosque. I want to find the oldest bookstore in Bombay. I want to unearth a dusty baritone sax in Calcutta. The egg curry has disappeared. And on the last slurp, I realize my drink had ice.

The holes in my shorts are a purdah screen.

Somebody's advice was: Go to India and walk around the villages. Go to Pondicherry and see if you want to go back.

After dinner, on the mosquito roof, I smoke the world's smallest hookah. But forgive me—there's not a lot of complaining in India.

Each day, the postcards bought in Khajuraho get hotter. I buy a second pack to make up for the ones I mailed, and then fantasize over the curves of ancient stone. But not on the overnight bus to Bombay, God no. Get in, lie down, hold on, pray. Each bunk crammed with four or five people, except for mine. I fall asleep in accidental blackouts, only to be jarred awake by a screaming, combusting truck outside the bus's foil wrapper, within arm's reach, its horn held down in a Doppler slap.

A shared Jeep seats 18 people; its seatbelts were long-ago ripped from the frame. I hand a banana through the window to a pleading woman as the Jeep pulls away from the curb. These roads: I'm more nervous about the next 24 hours than I am about the next 20 to 40 years. A nice reversal. Smoking seems to be the only time I take deep breaths.

I pride myself on how fast I close a menu. Gobhi, baigan, mutter, aloo, been there, know that. And I still avoid places where the waiters wear tuxedoes.

The Mumbai movie's intermission is the Interval. A DJ plays Mylo's *Drop the Pressure*. Plays Laid Back's *White Horse*. The Australian with four bracelets, flip-flops, and a scarf pulls out *The Economist* and catches up. Hector jets from New York to Mumbai. Two days later, we wake at 3:50 for the 5:30 train to Goa.

Goa's a place to tell your best friend your deepest secret. I drink ambiguous clear indigenous booze, the second choice. Kaju Feni sold out. What am I doing here? Where's the story? What needs to change? What am I missing? What's the point? I recoil with every swig.

A fur-hatted Irishman makes the case for keeping the dregs on your nightstand. When you get home, grab the bottle, swig, sign off *GARRRRIGHT!!!*, and pass out.

Too many travel icebreakers insult the host country. *Did you / Did you have to / Did they _____ to you too?* The beach kitchen cooks on one burner. I was the Senior Driver at Oliveri's, high on the pizza ladder. And she says, "In a place like this, how can anything be bad?" Ask the dead woman in the waves.

Hector's after-breakfast itinerary: "Gonna stay in here and drink water until I drop a massive deuce, then whatever." We're nearly dry after the last night in Mumbai, Maria Lodge, where Lefty mowed down our stash.

Basic Rental Accommodations: Lean-to, cabin, hut, shanty, tent, teepee, wagon, rock formation, cave, house, boat, igloo, treehouse, platform, tunnel, bunker, warehouse, factory (w/waiver), river island, roof, berth, locker, prayer chapel, wigwam, longhouse, lighthouse, room in a hallway of rooms, chains of halls you get lost in with a pool above you and a nightclub below.

Heard from behind a window grate: *I hate bananas!* There's an investigation in progress. Scarlett is dead. The Anjuna infrastructure is classified as camping. And we're two guys yelling *ass to ass* into a Goa pay phone like we've achieved a longtime goal.

Show me on the map where the raw sewage of Florida flows.

And Hector says, "I booted in Leopold's, on top of crapping my pants, which was the real highlight of the night. And you and Lefty were sitting upstairs, trying to force the chili chicken on me..."
And I say, "It was good, man, if you had it, you would know."
"If I had it, all of Leopold's would know."

Brother Rapp on the Baba Lodge stereo: Rolling once again with James Brown.

Please don't ask me on the lie detector: Were you ever the judge of bong-building competition?

The secret to ruling the world: Everyone wants a free slice of pizza.

The transportation hierarchy: Royal Enfield, bike, moped, bicycle, foot, taxi. Carried to a rave a day. Fueled by the fifteen rupee breakfast, a sleeve of biscuits and dirty chai. We've been warned of the surprise search. Undercover detectives are everywhere.

She wears: Rainbow bikini top, arm-wrapping tat, army belt, olive green butt shorts, orange-purple scarf harnessing a windmill of blond dreads. She says in a California accent: *He's this guy I met. He works on cars...* The man sitting with her says in a French accent: *Why you do this, you do not change, the same thing and the same thing...*
Later, the dealer says, "Follow me at a distance."

CHEESE IN SPACE! I raise my beer to the father of two small boys on their way out of the rave. Unsaid: Like what you're doing, man.

No mirrors in Goa.

And the man whose moped I will ride at 3 a.m. says, "If I were a DJ, I'd call myself North Pole. Cause you can never miss it, yeah?"
The dude on the Enfield with the head tattoo and long dreads, shirtless, all tats says: Nothing and everything at once.
The man who smuggled Molly from Berlin to Goa in a tube of foot cream says, "I want to push it to the limit."

And here it is, drunk on the moped, our first leaning sandy-surface turn in front of a bus...

I wake up on the beach at dawn with a policeman's hand in my pocket. And by some stroke of luck, have nothing. Our crowd, unsearched, watches while watched by the policeman's partner.

The morning swimmer says, "Let me hide my shirt in this palm tree."

Need to get in shape? Go to Goa and dance.

I haven't written a single postcard. The guys who work the hotel sit crammed at the bar watching WWF all day. I'm not saying we don't know what we've got.

Written in my notebook beneath a mess of math: It's OK to focus on the economics of it.

What do you have to do to spend 110R on a Kingfisher? It's the last day in Goa. Let's try to push out a lucid thought.

Hector recalls pledge: "It was the first time I'd heard System of a Down, and I lift up my blindfold and there's a severed cow's head. And I'm being asked—no, told—to kiss it." This is half-Indian Hector, mind you. Horrible he still feels sick. No drinking, no eating, nothing. Plain rice, jam toast. Maybe dal. No more.

What do you do to see your worries? How can I do yoga with warts on my feet? Every now and then the sea will rise up. He was pressed underwater face-first into the top of a coconut tree for the entire length of the tsunami wave, and lived to tell the tale. Now he splits his time between Goa and Antarctica.

Read the Rig Veda, imagine you're leading the ritual.

We continue south. I trim the beard in the dirtiest mirror in Kerala. We find a bar in Trivandrum: A candle-lit basement of men drinking room-temperature beer.

Mysore, my first day alone since Mumbai. An overboard special Thali, banana leaf hand-scooping with strangers. Got my glasses tightened, but need to tighten them more. Went to a beautiful bookstore—too bad I have too many books in my bag already. Will hit the Hampi trade scene after I survive this non-A/C, non-sleeper, reclined seat, spring-right-in-the-crotch gone-shocks bus ride.

Who is the nerd dude holding a frayed wire that disappears into a gray box on the side of a sharply winding mountain road?

Hampi at breakfast: Sweat running down my stomach. A man in a Cub Scout hat lifts a handful of flutes: *Music!* I check out the Balcony Lady in the barbershop mirror. Hampi: Pronounced Humpy. I receive: Haircut, beard trim, coconut oil scalp massage, neck massage, back massage, head slaps, nose wiggles, and eyeball swirls. It's hot as wool pants with long johns.

All the hand-painted signs. Printing exists on only so big a scale. All the burping. The waiter who stands over the table and burps, the woman on train who turns away from her husband (and into my face) to burp. All the beard. There's beard patrol, and then there's Serious Beard Patrol.

From the States, India is a step toward the wilderness. More dust. Families grow up on buffalo milk. People pick bugs from their bodies—but that's anywhere.

Under the mango tree: I want a mango to fall on us, but only where it would be a lucky close call. It doesn't. Instead, I destroy a thali.

And the innkeeper says, "Are you enjoying your holiday?" I'm trying to get a handle on it.

Why is Hampi built like this? Is it a pilgrimage site? Where do the pilgrims end up?

You say a year, I say three months, two months, six months, two months, a year...

The breeze from the exhaust fan of the temple's inner sanctum smells like bong hits in a Subaru parked at the dam. Fire, bell, clarinet, temple: Circles in the night.

It's morning again. Saturday plans: Check out the elephant. Eat. Do the tour. In my wallet, the receipt remnants of an almost threesome. You can be anyone you want with a pair of sunglasses.

Can banana porridge be considered Indian? And is it me, or after two days of good tips does this porridge have a surplus of banana?

It's a feat to wear white in this land. The cylinder of my Bic pen has never been so dirty.

Hector leaves for Bangalore, I stay in Hampi an extra day. To attempt sex. Just before noon, under the mango tree (again): My leg hair defeats a red ant. Walk in the afternoon, thinking about sex, yet buy *The Synthesis of Yoga*. My bag is too heavy with books. I have nine hours left in this ruined city before the overnight bus. How can I find a willing partner? Change tack entirely—cougar hunting? And once again they're bringing out the candles (and the bugs), another power outage, and if I only had a lady with whom to share this candlelight dinner. Somebody said there's nothing sadder than a man dining alone. Clarification—there's nothing sadder than a man dining alone, checking his watch.

The driver yells *Last Stop!* and I wake up on the overnight bus alone, parked in Bangalore, everyone long gone. In my bus dream, a band: *Ronnie Screwvala and the Hand-Painted License Plates.* Soon after, on the way out of the Bangalore mall, I eat a single cookie that costs more than my usual 156g roll of Marie Gold (also marketed as Marigold, Mary Gold, and so on).

The 36 hour train ride awaits. Hector and I are headed north to Calcutta. Keep your Kolkata. Will I ever be this far south in India again? From Calcutta, the plan is Darjeeling, then east-west traversing until we break for Nepal.

Calcutta with its Manhattan vibe, yellow taxis aiming for you, 30 people watching a movie on the corner. Old and smart. No Bollywood glitz. A newspaper headline seen over a shoulder: Schwag moves up to 12th place. Are people surprised when I pull out a US passport? Doubtful. Do I want them to be? Yes.

A store full of guns. I ask, "Can foreigners buy guns?" No. "Thank you." And Hector says, "If anything goes down in the next three days with a gun, the cops are going to go to that guy, and he'll say some foreign guy with glacier glasses came in and asked if foreigners can buy guns."

Do you consider a non-veg dinner daring?

At the government office: The guy helping me is training two guys, leaving the desk to take calls on his mobile, making multiple carbon copies, writing an official letter to me, addressed to my hotel room.

Across the room, bell-bottom trousers and a big brown collar: the security guard with his back to door, chatting and chai-ing it up.

Shamefully, I sneak my malaria pill.

Don Giovanni's 24 Hour Delivery: Pasta Pizza Chinese

You know the dinner will be good when you see the cut limes, the hot green peppers, the pickle, the pickled onions, and the typo *snakes* for snacks. Peter Cat: Fish masala with a leopard-print mustard marinade. And then I pushed it with the pickled onions.

Ganja-stuffed beedies: Once in the day, once in the night. And now the Swiss Army knife has been incorporated into both ends of the smoking routine.

Do you play the backpackers' see and be seen game? Do your eyes wander across foreign faces at breakfast? Do you exclusively employ *Suno!* Do you know the difference between *sunyee* and *suno*? Do you know when to use Urdu instead of Hindi?

Going today to check out an imported sax. It's April now. It's April and I have shit in my eye.

For those whose luck hands them digestive distress on the weekend of the Sunderbans safari: A small sign in the big boat's washroom asking guests to not soil the seats.

Calcutta car horns: A little like Holst. I give money to kids so they can grow up to be pizza guys. Gupta Brothers Sweetshop: Goop, there it is. You should be able to look your God in the eyes.

After putting the oversized cube of paneer in my mouth, I turn to the window beside me, where faces are pressed against the glass, hungry and glowing with life.

Step aside for the too-cool family, all speaking English, two brothers with flying collars, edgy saris on their wives.

The condom perpetually in my pocket is getting beat-up and dicey. Not counting couples, what percent of tourists have unprotected sex with an Indian citizen? A guess: 8%. Another guess: 13%

There's a billboard for a pen.

Found a gun: Hector and I pop balloons with BBs on the Maidan. And now a phone call must be made to the Oberoi Grand. We search for bottled water that meets a particular standard. We need a word for purified, oxygenized, UV-treated good-to-drink water.

Contrary to signage, no one cares what happens in an Indian bathroom.

2. Darjeeling

With no airflow on the A/C bus, you either hold 'em in or feel criminal. I ask Hector, "One hour left?" Five hours left. And then the windshield falls off.

What is Darjeeling? A bit more upscale, Wes Andersony. Take my word for it: There are snowcapped mountains right there behind the clouds.

Glenary's is pumping the slow jams. Hector orders: Fresh lime soda, salted (for the stomach), tandoori chicken half (dry for the stomach), one naan (for options). I order: one murg musallam (for adventure), plain rice (naturally), one glass of red (tasting like Walmart wine).

Done: The Most Insignificant Deal in Darjeeling. And the Most Insignificant Deal turns out to be WAY TOO STRONG. Something in it for sure. Now I know why those kids could barely stand and had no concept of ears beyond the face in front of them. Police are everywhere. Gorkhaland is marching, striking, ready to explode. They're smashing car windows. The Army base at the foot of the mountain is getting antsy. And the snowcapped mountains finally popped out.

The mountaineers wear their snow pants around town. What's it like here the night a big expedition returns?

Sometimes you see it, sometimes you don't. Most times you don't: The mountains and whatever else.

Tonight, a table for four on the balcony. We shuffle chairs for five minutes trying to find a view for everyone. With a new notebook you can tell people it's your first week.

Didn't happen: The Double Darjeeling Carpet Cleaning.

Stealing street style: Do you look for people you want to look like?

On the baldest tires in West Bengal, the taxi coasts in neutral down to Happy Valley Tea Plantation. Say it with jazz hands: Happy Valley Tea Plantation. The happiest tea in Happy Valley: Superfine Tippy Golden Flowery Orange Pekoe 1. After talking about tea all day, I know I know nothing about tea. Except *Galaxy* is the most expensive cup of tea on the menu. This is where Tea Lover Magazine sends reporters. Goodricke Tea House: The Ben & Jerry's of Tea. Do you bring a snakebite kit to the tea plantation? *Yes.* Did you see any wild snakes? *Not to my knowledge.* How many kilos of tea do you buy at once?

The fashion family is up from Calcutta: Loud talking, stitch strutting, sun-shading.

No ceiling fan, finally. That kind of place. Vermonty, Zermatty, Aspeny. All day with the bells of the clock. And Mr. Giggly Red Eyes says, "No, I swear—it's the mountain air."

Spotted: A clean, swept, solid garage.

I lie in bed because I got up at ass o'clock in the morning. And just before ass o'clock, I say *Screw it, it's 3:30, I might need the extra time.* And I went and sat on the can by flashlight and heard the alarm I'd set for 3:45. So the new alarm is for 9:15, about an hour from now. Pre-dawn, we Jeeped to the top of Tiger Hill and watched the sun eject from what we thought was clouds, what was red because of clouds, but was mountain. Because of the invisible land, all you see is a flat-bottomed cusp, like a bagel out of a toaster, and were we craving bagels, with two New York City women, one real-deal couldja-believe-it actual-factual writer. With a book! They were not into India but (maybe unknowingly) embracing it nonetheless, they bought the onion crisp breakfast fried chip-thing and said *Oh, that's gooood*, and *Yeah, it's a potato pancake or something.* India will take it as a compliment. Too bad they fly out tomorrow night from here to Calcutta to Bangkok, the Nepal trip scrapped, done with the subcontinent. They came to have their minds blown. They drop constant images of explosions into their descriptions of the experience. *We came to have our minds blown, and they were. Were they ever.* And *If these cars don't start moving, my head is going to explode.* So yeah, there, on Tiger Hill, watching the sun, sipping the free chai, I yearned for a bagel. There's so much yearning in India.

What goes on in the mind of the bug in my bed?

Hector leaves for Kashmir tomorrow; I'm staying here. Pineridge Hotel in the Ajit Mansions. Ajit Mansions: Where the pocks in the headboard are from rings and Rolexes. I've negotiated a bargain for nine nights. Because I know this location is good. Because I revised my budget after a hilltop purchase above town (where you know no one's spying from above). Because this room is red velvet. It has a light and a desk. A big bed.

Morning. I tell the kid at the hotel desk I'm going for chai. I don't find it, but pick up the newspaper, return, and read it on my room's chaise longue. Leave to find an ATM, any ATM, because I want a pocket full of cash if this strike heats up—and maybe some cookies—and the kid from the desk runs up as I'm halfway out the door. He says, "Tea! Tea, sir!" And behold a tray with a pot of chai masala. He thought I'd placed an order. Not the Darjeeling specialty stuff— is this a political statement? I put the ATM on hold, and sit in the ancient lobby and drink chai, and all the hungry, strike-stuck travelers pass the hotel entrance's panel-glass windows (18 in half the door alone) and see me scruffy, alone on an ancient couch, sipping. Ain't no Baba Lodge.

A good move has been made, one where the gut says fuck it, let's rock. I'm back in Room 130 for seven nights. Good. I didn't want to step down to the room across the hall, its baby blue fake carpet hastily laid (because if any carpet's going to be hastily laid...), its doctor's office furniture, courtyard view, scaffold-blocked windows, sad lamp and windowless bathroom with a palm-sized spider bent on revenge (during the tour, I missed it with my boot). But what am I talking about? Only the same stuff the protesters in the streets are—you need a place to live, to call home. It should be the spot that feels right.

The papers says the hills are on the boil. Again.

Back in Black floats in the window from down at the bar. Back in the Black. The new stuff—there's a lot of it. I finally don't have to use tobacco. A bit heavy. State College issue. And where did this jazz come from? And where did this jizz come from, you think, squirted awake on an overnight bus while freeballing in your board shorts. Tell me what action this refers to: Dam Jamming. *Would the Dam in question be a beaver dam?* Too many missed coincidences. Damn. There's only so many you get. And now I'll kick myself for it all night, and practice detaching, remaining silent. Regret. A tire iron to the insides.

Hey—your paneer's hanging out.

The mountains focus on drink, not food: Beer, tea, and a Jägermeister-like booze.

Drivers here are a little bit slicker. Sharper. Not necessarily stylish, but guys who know how to tie knots. Who could put the leaves into the dining room table.

Who sent spinach soup to my door?

The view from the water tanks atop the Pineridge Hotel is massive. The march builds to a fever below. What if this place erupts? Could it break into war? And speaking of explosions, will this cigarette reignite my bowels? Please no.

Down on the street, I jerk my head at the sound of fast feet: A pack of kids running. A man charges me and yells *Hey*— I dump my adrenaline. Turns out he wants to fight the man behind me. I'm on edge in Gurkhaland. (And waiting on the ATM...) You?

My key is heavy. Good.

The motto of the Central School for Tibetans: Others Before Self.

How to stay warm indoors in the Himalaya: Put on slippers, wear a hat, get in bed. The mountains draw on what I know from home, the knowledge that was useless everywhere else in India. It's kind of nice.

The desk kid delivers mint spinach soup and an onion-tomato-cheese toasty. He also gives me a new, working lamp. So I give him a nice tip. I missed him in the morning for the chai, mind you. I could get used to the daily routine. Paper and tea outside the door at 9 a.m. Dinner if I'm staying in, or entertaining. I understand how celebrities develop a reputation for their Green Room requests. And now time for desert. The call from the mosque starts up. Not exactly what I had in mind.

The beard, the massive beard. With a bandana on, I could be a bald bearded guy. Shel Silverstein. Pizza guys don't rock a lot of beards. And when I get home— *Look, I've brought a friend. Guess who's coming to dinner!* Opaque beard with a fishhook curl on the sideburns. Lot of open space under the lower lip, an ambiguous wisp in the center.

The desk calls to find out if I'm in the room: Hello? *Sir?* Yes. *Ok.* Ok? *Ok.* Thank you. *Thank you.* Bye.

A time-honored tradition: Hiding the waste. Radioactive, roaches, needles, scat, plumbing, septic, sewers, edits, Monsanto, Bhopal, Chernobyl, landfills, cemeteries, dumpsters, alleys, chimneys, getting the condom wrappers out of your car before Thanksgiving.

He only said *Keep fighting* to a man in the Gorkhaland march, but was captured by the Indian army as a subversive because the marcher was an undercover agent. He was grilled, tortured, and turned over to the US as a supporter of terror. It was just for moral support!

And now for the test of how cold the room is: Take a sip of water.

Conscious, what a word. Lucky not to think of it every day.

Do you read the newspaper with an atlas?

And because no part of my mind puts up an argument against *let's go to bed*, bedtime it is. Just a bit more chocolate to fuel the nightmare machine. I have water, a food stash, and a room. I'm rich.

Advice to future occupants of Room 130: Keep the curtains closed at night so if you bring someone back, they can ask, "Oooh...do you have a view?" And then you can open the curtains on the booming valley below. And so you don't feel exposed on arrival, so you don't have to stop and say *Let me close the curtains.* With its unsaid subtext: *Because I*

can't let anybody see me here with you, doing what we're about to do, because it's bad!
It's dirty! And who knows who might be watching!

New Dish (Sizzling Chinese Food): The waitress offers the Mixed
Grill at 140, the most expensive thing on the menu, and a little more than
I'm looking for. I propose sweet and sour chicken next, a reasonable
choice at 100. Nice round number. I ask for spice. Spice? Manchurian
Chicken, she counters, and she must be proud of it, because it's less than
the sweet and sour (or is it an inferior product at 90? Who cares?) Boom.
Sold. Chopsticks and fiery red. So it's me versus the Manchurian Chicken.
The texture of the chicken is real-deal lazy-susan Chinese, closer to duck.
Air-pumped. And damn, when you say spicy, you better be ready for
sliced chilies layered without mercy. Is this a boiled chicken? Good
Chinese food can make something as basic as chicken an adventure down
Weird Meat Street. Do you do delivery? I'm going to call. (This is the type
of place that has you planning your next meal mid-meal.) This dinner may
explode my ass. (A common sentiment these days.) I ask her if the
chicken is boiled. *No, not boiled, fried.* But it's so soft! *Ah, but that is our
recipe!*

Night in the Darjeeling market. This is where you meet people.
Maybe even buy things? Nope. I try to get what's not for sale. *I want your
hat, you have to bring it to my room...* Is the want-want world of the
marketplace where all of Darjeeling's courtship goes down? Where things
get said? *This shawl, it has to stay warm when it gets wet.* Warm and wet. That's
what I need. *Is it?*

Power outage! Dark! Dark in Danfay Munal, yet another Chinese
restaurant. A fellow diner deploys the headlamp. And I ask, as always,
how many of these are spontaneous couples? Candlelight now. This is a
town that demands a flashlight in the pocket. Are we back to camping
comparisons? In Darjeeling, it's not a comparison. Consumed some
Bollywood today after lunch. A backstabbing extravaganza packed with

23

men slowly stepping out of expensive cars, putting on or taking off shades, plot development via zoom in, twenty camera angles per staredown, a bit of horseracing, amateur extras, man-on-man slapping, billowing biceps, six main characters played off of each other in every possibly permutation, three hours of fury. I bought a cheap seat and moved up to the leg-roomy executive level. Antisocial behavior!

I live the life of a dictator-in-exile (complete with piles of marked-up newspaper clippings) in the Pineridge Hotel's best corner room. Room 130 with the chaise longue. And I'm starting to get serious about What Will Keep Me Warm—but I can find that in Nepal. While acclimatizing. When I know exactly how much room I have in my pack. The 500 rupee wool jacket is tempting, though. Damn tempting.

Who am I? A pizza guy in India. A bracelet maker. Owner of a Big Weed Stash. A boozer. The guy who eats with a pen in his hand. A cheapskate part-time scoundrel. Question asker. Respectable tipper. Another human afraid of the future. Ready to pull Spanish out of my pocket. Lonely. Cautious. Bewildered. A rhymer. A New Yorker. An Eagle. A raider of the night.

I worry the flickering candle will trigger an epileptic seizure. The city's hidden hundreds of stairs will pop my heart like the college classmate with the "minor heart issue" who collapsed and died after towing his sled to the top of the hill. I worry. But I hope I'm getting better.

And will All. You. Brits. Please. Stop. Calling. It. A Torch. But what's it to me. Keep on keeping on.

I'm an anarchist in the gas department.

The shawl, I get it now. A fat scarf that leaves your arms free. The original blanket scarf.

EMERGENCY! PAAN JUICE FROM A TAXI DRIVER WINDOW PRE-DATE ONLY PAIR OF PANTS.

Wind is blowing tonight and it's frigid. I put on my fleece to test the warm-when-wet theory. I should deck out in all wool for Nepal— wool vest, jacket, and shawl. Those big fuzzy yak wool socks. Pants? Sure. Wool underpants! Don't skimp, grundle it out.

I'm glad I'm getting to see some bad weather up here in the mountains before Nepal. A bit of a shakedown. Start with extra gear and be willing to give it away. Where can I get one of those 1930's scout-style head wraps? (Later I'll learn the word: Namlo.)

Darjeeling is already on to skinny jeans while the rest of the country wears flares. The men wear sweater vests and polos, shades and spiked hair, hoodies, and flat brim hats. The women wear train-tunnel eyeliner .

Wang-Den doesn't like Haldiram's or Hajmola, he prefers crushed Ramen with the spice pack stirred in. It's a political thing.

Imagine being an animal who can't wait for nightfall. Wait. I am one.

On the third day of the trip, in Delhi, I run for the bus as the ticketman leans out the door yelling agRA, agRA, agRA, agRA, agRA! I bang on the side, it stops, I climb on, buy an extra seat for my bag, and the bus fills up. With an armpit on my head, dust in my mouth, I scramble open an eight ounce ziplock bag, fill it with vomit, then fill another. I drop the bags out the window, down the side of the bus, hear the splat, and ever since have had the feeling it would come back. That's why, walking between the taxis tonight there was the *chiiiiiis* sound of a paan jet—*damn that was close*—and under the next streetlight found brown all over my pants. Not only liquid, but tiny chunks, the stain as big as a bratwurst, bits of it on my fleece, too. At the next food stall I got newspaper square napkins, rubbed off what hadn't soaked in, went to the pharmacy, and bought a Sprite and a bar of laundry detergent because, yes, I had to meet a woman in fifteen minutes and I only have one pair of pants. I washed them and tried to dry them with palm friction—no way. I hung up the pants, and went out in shorts like a chump. The next day, I took the pants to the roof to dry on corrugated sheet metal in the sun (the way clothes dry all the way down the valley) and now the pants are back to fine. No harm done. Regular old karma. And though I think I got them clean, I still see a bit of a brown stain (The Brown Stain!) and have to regularly convince myself I didn't whiff stale tobacco rising from my thigh.

I change my plane ticket to the last day of my visa, then shop for a wool hat. With a choice between black and tan, I buy the warmer one. Walking downhill through the bazaar is the closest I've ever come to playing fullback. I'm not traveling, I'm Italian, and my eyes are always cloudy as marble.

Kicked a pen the other night. It's nice knowing I had it from new to dead. It survived the road and died of natural causes.

Oh. My. God—New Dish! Surprised again, ordered mixed chow mein, beef/egg/pork, the egg a perfect greasy hangover-buster, the pork cubed with sharp edges I cut my teeth on, the beef shredded. Got to love places where the more you go, the better it gets. Apply hot sauce until the plate looks like a crime scene.

The Darjeeling soup you salt yourself, because in the mountains some people need more salt than others.

A real sprint to the finish line there, going piece by little piece with the chopsticks until it's only a few scraps of noodle. Downing the soup, thinking *it's broth, it's good for you, it gives you what you need, so eat it!* Scraped the bottom of the chili pot tonight. And how much of it is because I want them to see me eating this way?

Yes, those are lemon chunks at the bottom of the tea. What do you do with your one and two rupees? I buy snacks: a cookie, a banana. Though up here though I don't eat as much fruit. It isn't as in-your-face as down south.

You buy the chance to freshen your mouth when you pay the dinner check. If you don't pay, you leave with an ugly mouth. They hold back the seeds as collateral. You call for the bill to get fresh.

People sing and scream in the kitchen over *Smooth Operator*'s sax. Where was the last place you heard that solo?

In Goa, the beer was almost an afterthought. Here we mix heavy metal with Royal Challenge. Kingfisher Strong tastes a bit soapy. I'm crazy on custard, ambrosia rice pudding.

My pre-planned bribe intro: *Hold on a second, I need my first aid kit...I have something you might be looking for...*

Do you keep your window open despite the scaffolding outside?

When you accidentally pull a condom out of your pocket at lunch with a lesbian: *Not for you.* "You carry it around, just in case?" *You know, you meet people.* She nods in agreement.

If I ordered a pizza, it'd be headed for Ajit Mansions 130. AJIT MANSIONS! "Yeah, I met this guy, he lives in the Mansions..." I want the shawl-seller to tell that to her friends. *With a southwestern view*, may I add. The writing desk is where it should be. Corner of the room, next to the trash and the toilet.

This may or may not be the site of the old Drum Druid Hotel. I open another room's door with my key to compare the quality. There's a suitcase exploded on the bed. I get out, fast.

After trying on the peach-colored long johns, I fold them and tie the bundle with string, and take them back to trade for black. They look too much like my flesh gone baggy.

An Indian Air Force fighter jet buzzes Darjeeling. To say?

The Primordial Shithouse: Do you get the urge to take pictures in bathrooms?

Back to New Dish for the last dinner in Darjeeling—the type of mountain grubhouse where you keep your coat on. A family is too close for me to gas! The son, their only son, wears a sheepskin jacket and corduroy Dockers. Dad drinks a Kingfisher. They order the mixed grill, and it sounds like the wife is lobbying for an additional chicken mushroom. No dice. Have to leave early tomorrow, need to pack when I get back to the Mansions. I'll do up the moneybelt in the morning. I have a full load. Back to Delhi, 36 hours. Where in Delhi? Need to get directions over the phone. Fast. Tonight? Maybe.

A couple walks in, and it looks like the first date. "So what do you want to do?" *I was thinking greasy Chinese and some lovin'.*

You understand more than your brain is supposed to understand.

I'm on my way out of Darjeeling, searching for a shared jeep down the mountain, moneybelt strapped and safety pinned to the boxers. And how do I feel about this tourist scene in Glenary's? Take a guess.

Damn, the week went by (went buy). People say the party's in Southeast Asia.

At the next table: "In the U.S. we have lines on the road and everybody stays in their lane and nobody honks." And I turn and say, "Excuse me, sir! *You* are not from New York."

Is it a good strategy to stuff yourself full of food when you're on the cusp of something? Screw it, this warm chocolate pastry has me back at Pop's Donuts in Wolfeboro, pre-dawn, stocking up for a day of bass fishing in a rented aluminum boat.

The eroticism of the Khajuraho postcards increases in proportion to the duration of celibacy.

Mountaineering: Today's seafaring.

Can you smell the difference between southern and northern incense? Do you buy Hajmola to sate your cravings? And to bring them on? What if the Gorkhaland folks started robbing tourists to fund their rebellion?

There's always been somebody lost, wandering the earth alone.

How's India so far? It's good, but it could use a few napkins.

New Jalpaiguri Station, 3:13 p.m.: Sweating balls in big socks, boots, pants, goddamn moneybelt. Over there—is she the only one not married? I can't make out a red dot in this backlight.
Out of Gorkhaland, back to India, back to dirty hands, food hands, fingers piled with food being shoved in the mouths of babes. Americanesque potbellies. Kids pulling whole bottles of Thums Up through straws pinched in their chubby fingers. I already miss

chopsticks—they shrink the average bite, give pinpoint precision, don't taste like metal, aren't a hand. Straighten up, look sharp—the machine gun has entered the restaurant. Literally. An HK submachinegun wearing a local cop.

He was the neediest niceguy on the Northeast Express.

If the U.S. were India, trinket hawkers would crutch through jam-packed Amtraks, and a platinum lady would lean out of her bunk and ask with an Alabama accent *How much is the Baby Jesus?*

The pizza pilot is a small-town fighter jock, rocking the right stuff, second only to the snowplow driver. The Indian man I tell this to says: *Pizza supplier. You are pizza supplier.* All those hours behind the wheel imploring the snowflakes to Give The Drummer Some now lead me to give 100 rupees to each of the 17 year-old turquoise-vested curved-stick-blazing march-leading drummers. Leading Hector and I to the wedding of one of his mother's tertiary relatives.

Do you hit the wedding buffet and think *This is the real deal?*

Career goal: To be Kanpur's King of Paneer.

The wedding: Serious fatrolls in attendance. We passed a village wedding on the way in. I said, "Is that it?" And Hector said, "Yeah, I don't think so." Here the stage is as big as a basketball court, and guards are prowling with shotguns.

Pizza guy's biggest enemy is the clueless customer who parks in the designated driver spot by the dumpsters. It has enough room for two cars, you and the other driver, to whom you give a Top Gun thumbs up if he arrives as you're gearing up to launch from the lot. Gun it in reverse and whip the wheel 180, no brake, let first gear take care of the change of momentum. Only brake if there's snow on the ground so you spin. The best words you can hear are, "You're back already?" from the beautiful dropout who works the register.

3. Pokhara

We made it to Nepal, we're prepping for the Annapurna Circuit. First impression: the beers are colder. I sit on the sidelines of the soccer game (with all the other guys who wear glasses). The country smells almost as clean as Upstate New York.

How long has it been since you checked your email?

Nepal is an opportunity to reconnect to my Boy Scout roots. I wear what I used to wear on campouts. White t-shirt, cargo shorts, boots, dirt. Bought the scout-green wide-brimmed hat at the store, despite the embroidery *Nepal—Top of the World*. Which now I've come to like.

There's a drink on the menu called *Angel's Tit*. I could go for one of those. Maybe two. We compare planned expenses for after the trek. Hector: tattoo, whitewater rafting, and paragliding. Me: Hash and who knows.

At the Busy Bee Cafe: I want to be the hard, calculating, ice-screw-turning, frosty beard summit-team-leading motherfucker at the corner table who, when everyone else gets up to dance, locks his jaw to the bassline and his hand to the beer. And then the drummer steps in a funk beat and his grin comes out.

And I say to Hector, "The days of complaining about foot odor are coming to a close. It'll be an integral part of our existence for the next month."

And Hector says, "I gotta drop the bomb on the freak crew."

"Did you just reference Trouble Funk regarding your deuce?"

To pledge Delta Sigma Delta, the dental school fraternity: Only eat Sour Patch Kids for a month, no brushing, and open your bottles of beer with your teeth. The Pledgemaster says, "Don't worry, we'll have you fixed up by finals."

We drink to the point where we talk about life trajectories. "Don't question where I'm headed. There's no degree. No route. I come from a long line of people who packed up and took off. It'll be fine."

Clouds heavy. We're in the Himalaya and haven't seen the Himalaya.

The Busy Bee band observes the time-honored tradition of blazing at the set break.

When was the last time you listened to Santana covers with wrestling on the TV behind the band?

This trip: Learning to be lonely.

The ideal souvenir: The kind of thing you find in your grandpa's desk, and say, 'Damn. What a badass. Look at the year—'08, man! '08!'

A man with a mushroom haircut and aviator glasses (not sunglasses) gives yoga instruction to the maids in the Pokhara hotel's backyard, and I bet he's thinking, "Get y'all limbered up for some good Florida-style fuckin'..." What's the overlap between yoga, sex, and travel? Is this a takes-one-to-know-one type of thing? Do yoga masters come here for contortable partners?

And Hector says, "Where's that bus of geezers going?"
"Hell."
"Jesus, man, what's happened to you?"

And the class in the garden below has grown to eight, and the notepad is overrun with ants. A wilderness thunderstorm is brewing, and out of nowhere I have the urge to paint it. The local bad boys are roundhouse kicking leaves off the top of a small tree. Note to self: Don't fight.

My glasses are too tight. This is the unpredictable variable: a tenuous eye situation, outcome unknown. Heavy Chinese-made clip-on shades, ill-fitting Bombay frames riding a good centimeter above the ears (maybe only because my ears are sore), glacier glasses of limited use due to a reduced supply of contacts (another one lost this morning). Nerd alert! Not looking so badass anymore. But the mountains are not a place to be image-conscious. So I say to Hector, regarding his can of Axe body spray: "You're bringing that shit?" "Yup." "Good luck. That's how you die." No joke! One gram too many in the pack. *He didn't quite make it...*

Ants work day and night, right? Or do they sleep? Do these rainstorms drop snow on the Annapurnas?

A serious badminton party in the backyard our hotel shares with the house behind us. Thirteen people between the ages of 22 and 2, including a couple about to leave the runway of flirtation. UN jeeps on the road. That kind of town. The sheet aluminum roofs are held down with rocks, and these are the lakeside cottages. The good real estate.

Monkfruit!

Here you can feel the countries pushing against each other: The big guys, India, China, and Russia. Nuclear tension with Pakistan, so that counts, too. Then the medium-sized mountain spots that go out of control every so often, Afghanistan and Nepal. Bangladesh is a little guy, next to all the other little guys, Thailand, Cambodia, Myanmar, Laos, Vietnam. On up, you have bigger, modern states and serious nuclear politics, North Korea, South Korea, Japan. Does Taiwan have nukes? Does Singapore?

Table graffiti: Live the life you love, love the life you live.

Kerosene lanterns hang around the terrace. Tola acquired. My pack is 10 grams heavier.

"So is this the place that bumps the reggae?"
"I think there are several."

Staying light is expensive—it forces you to buy in the smallest quantity. No volume discounts here.

Regarding the hot chocolate and banana pudding: I wish I had someone to lick this off of.

4. Annapurna Sanctuary

From Besisahar

The bus drops us in Besisahar and we walk. Toe issues, as expected. An ingrown nail on the left big toe is pinching. I operate on it at a bench. Will have to keep an eye on it. After five hours, a guesthouse perched over the raging Marsyangdi river. A fragile-lipped pencil-mascaraed Nepali daughter greets us at the gate, and we say *Sure, we'll stay in the first place in town...* It breaks the cardinal rule, but whatever. The clouds clear at sunset and the mountains say hi for a minute.

Syange: New Roads

At breakfast, we tried to eat at the porters' table: Thwarted. We didn't know the protocol. Now we've made it to Syange. Made a turn on the way without checking the map, boneheaded, and walked downhill too far to backtrack (but it's never too far to backtrack...), all because of a sign claiming *Way to Hot Springs.* Reached the springs in an hour and a half, found another bridge, and crossed back to the route we should have stayed on. Walked on an under-construction road the rest of the way. Boring compared to the prior stretch of hurdling ridges through three or four villages, but then again, it's shocking to see the conditions they build in. A few enterprising Jeeps passed us, and in turn we passed men with bundles of PVC pipe on their backs, 20 feet long, only lifted with the *namlo* headstrap.

The day has two hikes: One through the *himal*, and one through the dal bhat—white rice, secret formula lentils, and a surprise vegetable side. All you can stuff. At the end of dinner, I can remember where I started, but every twist and turn of the refilling blends into an overall impression, beautiful, grueling, not what I expected, demanding frequent rest breaks, surprisingly smooth, and so forth. And the dal bhat journey's not over till you punch in at the squatter and file the final report.

Not to be confused with Doll Bot, Dal Butt, Doll Butt, Dhal-Butt, Dull Bot, Dole Bot, Dull But or Dole Butt. Get out your Nepali dictionary.

Trail mix handfuls are like first kisses: They don't stop until you've had ten just-one-more's.

Tal: Cold Crossing

Yesterday Hector puked and rallied in Chamche. Possible dehydration. We ate veg noodle soup and made it up the mountain. Crossed certain-death footwide cliffs. Gained about 2,000 feet on the day. Crossed the biggest suspension bridge yet during rush hour, and continued to leapfrog mule trains and market squads the whole way up. The women knit as they walk the trail. We passed an army barracks and its machine gun nests. The last push was a steep climb over a rim, and beyond waited the town of Tal. It sits on the dry lake bed of…Tal. Tal means lake, and that narrows it down enough.

This season there's no footpath to Tal, so it was into the lake, clip your boots to the pack, and wade through a calf-numbing just-melted mountain river. We worked our hands along a towering rock face for balance. At one point, the rock wall bowed in to form a deep cave-pool, and we had to leave the wall and walk through open river. Ten feet from the wall, the current was nearly enough to make me fall, even with a walking stick. But the cold felt good on tired feet, and we shuffled into town in our sandals. We spun the prayer wheels as we walked through the gate, and flipped a flat stone to decide which of the two inns we'd stay at.

The innkeeper was kind, and the room far surpassed last night's rough-wood spider frat. New, clean wood, and cozy. A hot solar shower, a clothes line with pins. For dinner, the dal bhat packed vegetables, beans, potatoes, and pumpkin, and amazingly, cornbread. It's understandable we passed out at 7:45.

Bagarchap: Layering Up

In Bagarchap. Big mountains finally popped out. We've taken a hard left on the map and are now heading west, straight for the map's blue-white center. Caught a glimpse of Annapurna II after a quick storm. Its peak is surprisingly far away, but pokes above all contenders. We stopped purifying our water with chlorine. Apparently it doesn't kill cryptosporidium, but we've dodged the bug.

Arrived early today, early enough to wash socks. Sally and Joel are here, the couple Hector and I split a taxi with on the way from the border in Belahiya. They're cold. Yes, the temperature's dropping—my first day with long johns. Soon I'll layer up with socks and rain pants and wind pants and who knows what else. Peered in the window of the guesthouse across the street and witnessed a pizza in the making . Nepali phrases are accumulating.

En route to Chame, up and down and up some more. Resting now for lunch, waiting for the daily veg noodle soup. Why was Bill at the pizza shop such a good boss? Because as much as he wants to take care of the customer, he also knows when to say fuck 'em. Because he drives a Dodge Ram Hemi, has a house, bought his girlfriend a new Jeep, because he smokes copious amounts of ganja, because he's a solid worker, because he started out as a driver, because he still drives weekend day shifts, because he rocks the moustache, because we built a fire pit together. That's what I mean, he's open to ideas. He trusts me to take six-thousand dollars cash from his house to the shop in a paper bag. We talk about cars, first cars, best cars ever driven. Good to shoot the shit with. Because he offers to jump my car if it dies in the cold, to pull it out of a ditch with a chain if I slide in the snow. When I'm dry, he gives me homegrown for free. I bring over a case of Labatt Blue and we watch the playoffs, then I crash in my tent in the yard. In the morning I drive to Byrne Dairy through flurries and grab a box of donuts to go with our dozen cups of coffee.

Three weeks before the Super Bowl, I said to Bill, "I want to drive the Super Bowl," and he said, "We need three drivers, so you got it." I put a promotional scheme to him, said, "Let's make some Super Bowl specials, you figure it out with Ron and I'll post a Facebook ad and it'll be gold." So we did it, and sure enough we got a bunch of preorders, five pies, ten pies, wings too (damn, I could go for some wings right now), and then it was *go go go* all night, screw the sidewalk. Charging through snowfields, get in and get out, not without moments of confusion. Freshmen who didn't get their wings, rooms trying to put a $200 order on seven credit cards, and I'm fishing around in my vest pockets for their receipts, calling back to the shop, "Run this card, will you?" All sorts of errors, and I'm trying to manage the situation, be the diplomat—*your Super Bowl party is NOT fucked, dude*—and I think I made the most I ever made that night. Trying to catch the game on the radio between stops, switching my allegiance based on the wallet holder's jersey, and when I got back after the last run, after the top of the ovens was finally empty and our board didn't have a single yellow ticket, after the rest of the crew's beers had already been cracked, I finally had the beer demanded by pizza and wings. The beer you can't have while you're working (sure, you can drink the same bottle, but it's not the same beer) because it's the beer you can't have till you relax, the beer you have *to* relax.

That night the shop experienced the year's extremes of stress and release, marijuana in the kitchen after the owner went home, the first hit (for me, anyway) after a night bordering on a cross country race, an environmentally unfriendly biathalon, surprisingly not sponsored by SCCA, because when I get out of the car, I'm running, and upstate it's all hills. Yes, I'm the pizza guy who runs across the campus with the dirty red bag, who knocks you to the wall (nearly) while charging up the dormitory stairs, who shows up at your door out of breath and sucking wind, unable to report the total. I don't run in hallways—too connotative of structure fire, too great a chance of missing a mirror-spied towel drop through a cracked door. But in stairwells and outside, I'm booking it, which allows me to rock the t-shirt and vest all the way down to 32 degrees. Pants: I went six months with my utility jeans, usually boots, but saw the light when I drafted an expensive pair of Diesels into service. The pockets are tight enough to make the bank bulge ambiguous—*either a fat wad of cash or...*—either way, it's a win. Only resorted to snow pants one day, for the Valentine's Day blizzard. Again, it has its own Wikipedia page. Look it up.

Pisang: Rising Rock

We're next to the fire in Pisang, and now each night I wear the warmest clothes possible, though I can still get away with socks and sandals. The woman who runs the lodge has a smile you can see from half a mile away. The stone village is filled with kids in disintegrating sweaters and overalls. They skin-the-cat on fence posts and swing sticks at each other. Alert—just undid the neck zipper of my fleece, the wood stove is heating up. The hat's coming off next. The Russians are prowling for Smirnoff.

Today we traced a stadium of rock, a steep swipe of rock towering above the trail, sweeping along the river. It's so tall it still holds snow. From here at the lodge I can see it. At one point, we picked along a ledge, what I imagined, as a child, a mountain trail would be, what I imagined before I'd ever climbed a mountain. A balcony path of rock, blasted into the side of a sheer face, something straight from a *Road Runner* cartoon. A mule team passed us on the edge to keep it interesting. We know to hug the inside. How far can a mule kick a man?

The river became tiny below us. According to the map, the wall of rock rises 1,400 meters above us, about 4,500 feet. Skyscrapers, step down. And now we can look horizontally, unobstructed, to Annapurna II.

Straight across, I note the spot level with my position, and then raise my eyes to the peak—16,000 feet of mountain there. The tallest Adirondack peak can fit in its belly. You don't hop out of the car and scramble to the top. Not here.

The cold in this window-filled "Dinning Room" reminds me of the house we named Ol' Yeller, bundling up for breakfast, snow falling outside the window, and not falling on a city but on the corner of Eaton and Montgomery streets in the town of Hamilton, Madison County, New York, and snow falling on cut hayfields outside the barn on Washburn Farm Road in Glasco, Ulster County. Also New York. This is what walking does. All the places I want to walk! The Finger Lakes Trail, Hokkaido, Slovenia...

Manang: Skywalkers

Started with a backtrack to the high road: Over the Marsyangdi River, through Upper Pisang, then up and out along the side of the mountain to a thousand-foot straight-up slope marked with a zig-zag trail. We crossed a suspension bridge to reach the base of the trail, and stepping off the bridge we passed a trekker who had just descended. His advice: "Good luck climbing that."

Up we went, picking our way, stopping every few zigs for breath, feeling loopy as the air thinned. Reached Ghyaru at the top. Only old women in the village. Now above the treeline, the trail leveled out and hugged the mountainside, a thin footpath cutting across steep gravel slopes ending in cliffs. Slippery gravel. Before setting off, Hector gave the trail a blank stare and said *that looks excruciatingly dangerous*. And I guess it was.

The next village, Ngawal, was a bit more prosperous because it has a monastery. Or maybe vice versa. Far below, a joke of an airstrip (but no joke if you're in the plane). Then down a killer descent to Paugba, thinking *if only I had snow and skis.*, then through swamp and low bushes on the banks of the Chhetaji Khola, small trees and clearings like an abandoned campground. We rested at Mungi. Hector ordered "the bomb", a hot kati roll the size of an artillery shell. For me, a plate of fried potatoes with onion and lemongrass. Quality. The serving must have weighed five pounds. Then into the ponchos and into the rain to bang out the last hour up to Manang. Hector charged ahead in his usual stern stride, the angry dad stomp. I hung back, amazed at the color of my hands, brown and purple, tan and cold. My pack was pinching my neck and spine, something was off with the poncho. The usual end of a long day.

We arrived at a lodge in Manang, chosen for its new blue roof, and the innkeeper said, "No more shower, sorry." The solar shower's tank had been drained for the day. The town's water station was also closed, so we rehydrated with tea. In lieu of a second dinner, we went to the bakery and topped off with cinnamon rolls, chocolate Danishes, and jam cookies. Watched a movie at Manang's cinema, a stone hut with a projector and five rows of yak fur benches. The sleep was good despite a nightmare of bad guys strapping bombs to people's heads, shooting indiscriminately. They latched an explosive to my vest, but I flung it away at the last second to avoid doom. Eventually we paid our way out, though I had to drop the names of every Indian kid I went to high school with. They gave me a Turkish passport with only my first name, but I was somehow allowed to cross the border.

As much as I think about sex, this hasn't been the most spectacular year. More a year of reflection, and still nearly every morning I wake up and mentally rehearse elaborate plans of who I'll do what to, when I get to wherever. Futile! What is my relationship to acquisition? Even here, I don't mind seeing the mountains through the window at dawn. Sometimes it seems Hector's only motivation is to peg the peaks to a memory card.

Khangsar: Loose Goats and Other Delights
We're in Khangsar village, two hours up the Khangsar Khola from Manang, on the trail to Tilicho Lake. Goats own the town square. A nice

stacked-stone teahouse, and we're the only guests. Arrived around noon and have been doing this since: eat soup and crackers, wash socks, wash feet, sit on the bed and read *Leaves of Grass*, read *High Altitude First Aid*, rip terrifying gas (*Leaves of Ass*), walk the town in sandals, check out the roof, have tea and cookies, and now put in the dinner order, which will be served in an hour or two. Thankfully back to the dal bhat—all you can eat is all I need. Big walk tomorrow up to Yak Kharka.

We're here for acclimatization, 200 meters above Manang, 3,700 meters altitude. 4,100 tomorrow. Down and back up. Two trekkers cross the square, the first we've seen in town. Havoc now—someone's goat is loose. And here are two, no, three porters in sandals with six-foot diameter coils of black tubing on their backs. It's three-inch pipe, ten to fifteen rings of it. Heavy. The men of the town are gambling on the front step of the lodge (Hotel-On-Height) as they've been doing for the past four hours. I only have 14 iodine pills left. Should have bought more from Walmart back home. Maybe find them in Jomsom? Bottled water may come into play, but damn, it's almost two dollars a liter!

I could stay here a while if I had more books. It's like the Glasco barn. The weird vibe of the Hudson Valley: Kingston-Saugerties-Dutchess County, Woodstock even. Not the city, not upstate. Where you can find fancy things without trying too hard. Where you're linked to major transportation: New York State Thruway, Amtrak, Stewart Airport, the Hudson. Where you're close to Massachusetts, Pennsylvania, New Jersey, and Connecticut—and far from Canada. Where commuting to Manhattan is an option, no matter how masochistic. Where city people come to poke around, to consider, to try to write. Damn, I could go for a plate of Tom Cavallo's wings. Utica! Now that's upstate. Hot wings, good trails, thick snow, a wood stove. Should I settle down to the life of a pizza porter? Is that a decision somebody makes? I need more *she* in my thoughts. Peripatetic—peripathetic? Living in a three-walled room in a below-code barn.

Why didn't Chicago work out? Things could have gotten serious with Ashley from Boone, North Carolina. But you had to pack the car, sweating in the alley, and kiss her goodbye forever, right there at the bottom of the fire escape stairs on the last day of July like your visa's expiring, only one week after you met. So have faith. Forgive yourself. You're in backcountry Nepal in a no-phone village waiting for an all-you-can-eat platter of dal bhat that will constrain your ability to make new friends for the next 24 hours. You live a charmed life, my boy.

Shortwave radio and tea—it's a party.

TSW, Toy and Sports Warehouse. At one point in my life, the best place. The last time I was in a Toys R Us, maybe a year ago, I wept in the GI Joe aisle. *This used to be all it took to make me the happiest person in the world.* When did life get sad? What is there to do except keep on doing what I've been doing? Look forward. But my gut still sinks when I think of the years ahead.

If you stand over a wood stove your whole life, you die at 60.

Yak Kharka: Sliding Land
We climbed about 500 meters from Khangsar to the top of a ridge on the edge of town. The trail was nearly nonexistent through fields, and we used the topo map and compass, and sure enough we found the trail wrapping around the ridge. We followed it, close to the edge. Passed some yaks staring us down, and then we spotted the prayer flags marking a pinnacle. A knob of rock with mountains on all sides, more than we'd seen so far, and miraculously it was clear for photos and jaw dropping. From there, we descended another slope using a technique best described as skiing—the type of trail where you stand on the edge and think, "Shit, I gotta go down this?" I pulled open the telescoping second walking stick strapped to my pack (so far unused) and we dropped toward the blue hair snaking below. Twenty minutes later, we hit the landslide. A daredevil

ramp of gravel stretching all the way down to the river, four hundred feet below. A faint track crossed it where people had taken their chances. And now it was our turn.

One at a time—my first step sent pebbles all the way, all the way down. *Jesus. Alright. I'm going for it. I think the line of rock is stable.* I ran out, two steps, each slid, and then I landed on a solid patch. *Alright. Next gap wider.* I picked a downhill target, jumped out feeling again like I'm skiing, slide—slide—slide—each stride sliding downhill—then a patch of solid ground. I watched Hector, my walking stick extended toward him for moral support at best. He's a man without experience on skis. Slide, hesitate, slide—*he better not go down, come on—look where your feet are going—forward momentum!* And he leapt to join me on the island. We crossed the landslide's other half with the same slipping and sliding. Damn—we honest to God could have died. (I crossed myself before going. That's rare.)

The mountains demand respect. A porter passes the teahouse carrying three backpacks strapped together. Slow and steady, like we've been doing. We are on our way to Thorong La, we've been climbing the pass since we started, there's no way forward but over, and today's climb we hope will help us handle the altitude.

Where are the Ukrainians? Where are Fabian and Fatih? Where am I? Up in the middle of nowhere listening to Bollywood on a shortwave radio. A couple here at the teahouse watched us through binoculars today, waiting nervously until we crossed the landslide. Nice to know.

Nepali fraternity: They make you funnel hot tea!

Ledar: Operation Snowbird

Made it to Ledar, only an hour's walk. Dropped the packs, walked another hour out and back for the altitude exposure. On the other side of the Kone Khola, yaks graze on near-vertical slopes. It makes sense fallen yak is on the menu. Mostly cloudy today, and I wouldn't have wanted to try to cross the pass. We'll be up there two days from now, most likely. Things are chilled and windy. 4,200 meters, above the tree line. The wind whips up the valley and smacks us here in the—teahouse sunroom? Yes, the only semi-protected, public place in the lodge. Our room has thick red velvety made-in-China blankets. Although here in the sunroom, I can still see through the wallboards to the rock outside. Washing my socks out there in the cold took supreme willpower. I wish my gloves were here, not back in my pack. I'm wearing almost all available layers. My hands are gray-purple. Dreamt last night of driving a rickshaw around Hamilton, NY, and on across the country, fixing some plumbing (actual plumbing) along the way.

Trimmed the moustache. Sometimes I want to bag the wanderer thing and shop at Walmart, buying big bars of Hershey's Special Dark, hoping to meet someone (and knowing I won't), and above all relishing the money I'm saving. But still feeling hosed when the bill creeps over $60. A cheapster—who will accept me in America?

And from across the sunroom, she says, "Is this a word, con-temp-or-ann-ee-us-lee?" And now, despite her elevated bench and the boyfriend who had imbued her with a superior air, I know she's not perfect. I'm better at one thing than she is—comprehending *contemporaneously*. Ego! Could I teach college? *Damn, hombre, we've been through this...* I miss crashing those faculty parties, laying out the steaming pasta trays under the warm wood paneling, then out through the new snow to the car with an intellectual contact high, and imagining it all over again when finally walked into my rented house in the village, freezing at first, warm in a bit. I'll shovel the driveway tomorrow. What is that? I want the least possible obligation to superiors—always. Am I ready to accept poverty? Maybe. Obscurity? Doubtful.

Why not? Neither demands loneliness. Academia: farting up a storm in your little office. There must be a special pleasure to late nights in an empty limestone building. Pounding green tea and granola, grading papers, and doing exactly that.

It's official. Apple momos are the bomb. Little steamed apple pies, yes...

Hector pulls out the diminishing toilet paper roll and says, "I've smoked joints bigger than this—solo."

Snow on May 8: Just like upstate. It's snowing the snow I hate to drive in, the rattlesnake on the windshield snow, little rice pellets, frozen rain, the slushy sound sweeping under the car.

Thorong Phedi: Card Games
Another day. Waiting on the weather. Boonanza!

High Camp: Diamoxed
We woke to clouds covering Thorong Phedi lodge with visibility at 20 meters. The innkeeper said it was normal weather, but Hector didn't want to find out what was brewing a thousand meters above. So we bailed on crossing the pass. The weather cleared at 7:30, and we headed to high camp up a zigzag attic staircase. An hour's climb later, we're perched in the sunroom. The lodge is surprisingly warm and affordable. Not like last night's bill- buster momos. So we got the hardest part of tomorrow's ascent out of the way, and we have about two hours to the pass tomorrow—if the weather works out.

Gone in 60 seconds: My beef momos. The Swiss have arrived and have no need for a menu. "We have food coming," they say. Guess that's packed into the porter deal. Their jackets—Jack Wolfskin? More like Jack Foreskin. But it's nice to see some non-Nepali technical gear—the Swiss are equipped. We're at 4,880 meters (16,010 feet), Thorong High Camp, and *damn* I want to *eat*. All you can eat. I miss having a kitchen where I can dig around and put something together. I miss *Hardball* (because it's an excuse to hang out with my dad), I miss Walmart (*yeah, yeah, heard you the first time*), miss its Equate-brand goods. I miss splurging on Reese's Peanut Butter Cups during a long drive (with a coffee, oh yes). I'm a plain old American. How can I survive in the city? In any city?

The Swiss have gone back on their word and opted for the garlic soup. Smell it. And one says, "There's a bit too much garlic in here." Not something you'd hear in San Juan de Ortega.

Am I on the verge of burning out? (And is this all it took?) *What was the happiest moment of your life?* What a question to ask, and when would you ask it? Right now, I grudgingly accept I have to keep on living, seeking something tolerable through which I can pass the time. I could fall off the mountain at any moment—

Hector falls asleep on his back on the sunroom's bench with the map over his face.

The scuffed housing of my Canon Powershot SD800iS brings me back to when I worked in the Barnes and Noble café (not even a Starbucks, only "proudly serving" it), and I strained my budget to order the camera for $300 from Tiger Direct, and how it used to be so new and nice, so inspiring, and how I used to believe I would create real art with it, how I thought this little camera would be my salvation. Should I be wary of my next technology purchase? A laptop, by some miracle? Is right now better than retirement? A point for debate: Sacrifices.

It's 1:15 p.m. in High Camp's sunroom and I want tea tea tea tea tea... Whoa there—I had the urge to stand up and shout *I want to get out!* It *is* a crowded room up here in the rocks. I've extended the trip, I'm headed to Kathmandu. Have I blown my budget? I'll have to make it back to Delhi overland—it'll be well monsooning by then. This is the stuff that makes my head hurt, and it's not the altitude. I need an internet connection. I think I could be productive. Jesus, I'm hungry watching the Swiss feast. A head's worth of hairs have been shed into my knit hat (the black one from Darjeeling), and like every man, I wonder *Am I balding?*

I'm keeping tabs on the headache, watching for altitude sickness—stay with me now, this could be the first real conflict of these pages. Hector and I sing the Hallelujah Chorus, but substitute *Veg Pakoda!* Mint tea en route. What's the story here? Missing hot wings on Super Bowl Sunday. And the Swiss have the world's biggest tin of hot chocolate!

We sell a strip of Diamox pills. Hector says, "And now, for the second time, I'm selling drugs on the subcontinent."

Waiting outside: The Definitive Brick Shithouse.

You can only sit around and bash Western society for so long. Then you get hungry. Yes, I'm wearing gloves as I write this. Someone, somewhere has taken a Nalgene bottle up the ass. The sunroom is threatened by onion-garlic-egg soup farts. Hector dares me. I too would love to see the sunroom's reaction to one of these bad boys uncorked…

The factory writing on my aluminum water bottle says: Enjoy Basketball Sunny Sport Bottle.

And Hector says, "My God, I would kill for those jackets." The Swiss crew has matching blue and black down-filled hooded coats. I wish I had someone to carry my books. Screw it. We eat. So. Much. Are we burning all these calories? With the tea houses' lack of insulation, you bet. A zit is buried deep beneath the beard. Snow swirling outside the sunroom now, snow that makes you say *Look at that snow!*

Someone cracked the window: Snow in the room! Snow in the room!

The teahouse speculates on the action of Diamox. Does or does it not have side effects. It's a drug that increases the oxygenation of your brain. Of course it has side effects.

Spotted: the mountain guide who peeks at his face-down cards. The Swiss are onto another crazy meal. I say damn, did you traffic all that in here on your porter's back? *She's so strong she packs her porter on her back.* As annoying as choosing a ringtone at dinner. I have a two pack-a-day habit (of Bourbon Cream cookies). Hey man, sometimes a ringtone's the only music you get.

Is the Australian guy rocking a threesome with the two Israelis? You never know. Hitch up the blanket and put your legs by the heater. Go out in the snow in your sandals to drain.

Fellow trekkers: Stop complaining about the Nepali food. (Have I been?) We're damn far from a Walmart, and your top priority ought to be the cleanliness of those long johns. Everyone knows you haven't showered since Gorakhpur, and wet wipes don't count.

The devil is lurking in every seat cushion and itchy neck in this room, and you better cut those fingernails soon or risk permanent disfigurement. Everyone's popping altitude meds, washing it down with seabuckthorn tea. Half a pill doesn't cut it, and two will have you selling tissues at stoplights. And the tubes in my torso are torqueing, excuse me, and allow me to be excused before the whole shebang winds up on my permanent record. Because you need to look over your shoulder (for mistakes) and you need to look over your drafts (for dandruff) and you need to pull out the red pen before you make a baby with your administrator, the one with the giant safety pin in her long plaid skirt.

Thorong La: A Walk to the Jug

Icy pebbles. Hector and I pick along the trail to the pass, cold and shaking. *It's a sidewalk in Hamilton, NY.* We've walked on ice before. We can handle it, we got by upstate, 2,000 steps to downtown and back, on a mid-February Friday night, with four feet of snow on the ground and a storm rolling in, on a sidewalk walked by 1,500 people, downtown and back, and walked again the next night, tramping down wet fresh snow, and then there's a cold snap on Sunday night, and the path stays knobby and frozen and hard blue, and then you walk the ice while drunk on Monday night. So if you can handle that…

The high pass—a legitimate extreme environment. Would you live here?

Ma, I passed! I passed, ma, I passed! Hector and I smile weird beardy smiles beside the prayer-flag smothered sign: 5,416 meters. I pose for one holding my Boy Scout bandana—*this is for my homies.*

The Boy Scouts' approach to camping was slightly different from the REI/Sierra Club brand of "outdoor education". We used one-pole canvas tents stitched in the 1930's. We went to scout reservations, also pre-war, and the Scoutmasters marched us in a forest loop around the property. *We'll do a 25-miler on Saturday...* The philosophy is conservationist, but John Muir, not Greenpeace. High impact camping. The leaders—dads—attempted to maintain the appearance of order. The flag had to be raised and lowered at every campsite with ceremonial rigmarole. But despite the protocols, we trucked in 500-count boxes of strike-anywhere matches we had convinced our parents we needed for the trip, we dropped a burning ball of paper towels down the latrine (and Jeff pissed it out before disaster), and someone always fell in the river or jumped broadside into the wall of a tent at 2 a.m., someone always threw a D-cell battery in the coals. *Take cover!* Someone always walked through the fire and burnt out the crotch of their nuthugger scout pants, the can of pork and beans was always chucked off the highest cliff, someone always got a hernia trying to hump the cast-iron Dutch oven slung beneath their pack, and we always got soaked in a storm. Someone always brought a few cigarettes stolen from a parent, and we huddled behind a rock and passed them around, but most often we headed into the woods and got plain lost, the whole time wearing the pants. Scout Pants: 80% acrylic, 30% polyester, 10% wool (yes, I double-checked the math), the Pants force scrotal sweat glands into overdrive. Surprisingly comfortable when you buy them, traitors after the first wash. Tailored to display the progress of puberty. Luckily, scout pants also exist in sizes big enough for the waist of the dad who drives the 12-passenger van, and we bought those, and our mothers hemmed 'em up, and we maintained our skater image while conforming to the dress code (waist scrunched by the

51

webbed belt's sliding brass buckle). We carried a surplus of pepperoni. Oatmeal in the morning, provided no one tipped it over or the grill didn't collapse, and we were force-fed black coffee (more so magma) to prepare for the day's mission, and to send even the most stubborn colon on a double-time march to the grime-hole. We built our campfires taller than the lowest overhead branches, despite the Scoutmaster's ultimatum to not build them higher than our heads (*or I'll douse it, just you watch*).

Our caravans rolled up Route 22 into Putnam County, or up the Taconic (forever!), or up the Thruway on Friday night in a snowstorm (*with everybody and his brother!* cursed the father at the wheel), all the way to Camp Reed (or what was habitable of it in January: one log cabin with a wood stove) for two days of Gore Mountain and its ancient red gondola. Connecticut, Pennsylvania, and New Jersey be damned, this Headless Horseman patch says Westchester-Putnam Council, and we've got the gas money and the grit to bivouac anywhere in the Empire State. *Excelsior!*

They put guns in our hands, a small deviation from the granola approach. We never asked *Why are we learning to shoot?* Maybe for hunting, but more so for when China invades. BB guns, 22s, shotguns— automatics was where they drew the line. The dad in charge was in the FBI but he didn't look the part, which made him dangerous. Range shooting (with safety goggles, surprisingly), mostly into the hill behind the firehouse. There's no need to bring the entire arsenal on a camping trip. But we did. Tell you something else we did: Four guys in a tent jerking it in their sleeping bags, the camping-rough palm friction audible when quadrupled. No one busted a nut. The point was to prove it gets bigger, four tents in a tent. In the same spirit, we smoked cigars and let the campfire mask the smell of tobacco on the clothes. And all along, despite the scout pants, love was nowhere in sight. A few of us once went to a meeting of the co-ed, BSA-affiliated Explorers to see if membership might be worth it. Their only outing was a yearly ski trip to Colorado. Not enough fire. So instead we pledged allegiance to the flag.

Muktinath: Bobshaken

Beard Patrol: "You've got a little something over there—no, pinch it." "Ah, egg." And now it's Royal Stag, a Bob Shake, and a fatty at 10:37 in the morning.

Yesterday over the Thorong La—last to leave high camp at 6:01, the equivalent of leaving Thorong Phedi at 4:45. Around the first bend: ice. It was tricky on scree glazed by the night's snow, and I thought of high camp's caution flyers for frostbite. I held the bamboo stick in the left and the trekking pole in the right, and we inched forward and up, and up around the bend. A porter ahead almost lost his bag and himself into the spine-grinding rocks stretching down, down, down.

Weak ankles, weak knees, weak hips, weak back, weak shoulders, bad elbow, wrist pangs, arthritis. Joint pain, cracking knuckles, gnarled hands, crunching neck, bad neck, cracking neck, cracking jaw...

But we made it here, Hotel Bob Marley, home of the frothy green Bobshake. Their other specialty? Hash burn potatoes. It's Hector's birthday—we get both.

My first pizza delivery was in Chicago, pro bono, bringing Apart Pizza down to Irving Park Road, and *damn*. Thin crust, a 600 degree oven, and I was in there for the opening day's free-slice deal. They were playing Prince. Italian grocery toppings: artichoke, peppers, special cheeses, prosciutto, black olives, all on a thin, thin crust. THIN CRUST! New York fuckin' crispy City style. Thin crust, but filling. Satisfying in ways Chicago Deep Bloat can't dish out.

There was an old man geared-out in Ledar, and we caught up to him again at the last teahouse before the pass. He said, "Do you have an Ahltee-meeter?" And Hector said, "No, but I have a guidebook. Sixteen-thous—" And he said, "No, not feet! Meters! Tell me in meters!"

Close to the ground we eat momos. There's a momo shop that sells momos stuffed with the ground meat of dead climbers. We boozed and ate meat before visiting Muktinath, and Hector's Indian mom would surely be proud. And now we're onto RAMBO-brand Apple brandy. Branding gone mad? Or just wrong?

Upstate, there's a barn full of books called the Berry Hill Book Barn, and I have a book from the barn titled *Basic Mountaineering*, and no, it hasn't helped. Yet.

Once you cross the pass, you're not so much in the mountains as dominated by them.

We pick around the Muktinath temple and its surrounding rocks.

A sadhu calls me. "Come, sit down, you can sit..." He is 49 years old (twice my age) with ashes on his forehead, and rags and feces in his fire pit.

I say, "Do all sadhus smoke the chillum?"

And he says, "You want to smoke chillum? Ok, come here, sit down. Only charas, not ganja—I have to find a rock—" He plugs the rock in his funnel. He's from Himachal Pradesh, 12 years a baba, and he learned English in college. He mixes one Gurkha cigarette with his crumbly pollen and packs it to the top. And he says, "You light it."

I lose two matches trying. One left.

He says, "Let me." He lights it and cherries it up, a pro. Back and forth, back and forth, a never-ending cough fest, cotton cloth over the base as a screen. And boom, I'm peeling off layers and wishing I'd brought my sunglasses. I thank him and walk. A deuce coming on, the tobacco's fault. It's 5 o'clock. I stop and sit on a step, watch the trails below. How would I act if I knew this feeling came from mushrooms or mescaline? I breathe.

He passes me on the trail back down. I catch him, and we exit through the temple complex's secret side door. He invites me to see his cave. Thanks, but no thanks. Baba heads out.

I follow the trail downmountain. *When else will you get the chance to see a baba cave, at Muktinath no less?* His smudge of orange walks away through the rocks, he's nearly gone. I aim to intercept him, going Special Ops, off-roading, hopping from boulder to boulder. Catch him just before he slips out of sight over a ridge. Ahead is the cave, a tent of boulders, and waiting there is everything he needs—or everything he needed. Manure fuel, wool blankets, water jug, puja spot, ambiguous jars of powdered food, an empty McDowell's bottle (*sometimes it gets cold*, he says), and above, on the flat rock that forms his roof—the fireplace. Then another long, narrow cave with nothing in it. He says, "Good view over here." A flat stone he sits on, with a vertical stone jammed behind it, a rock-hard loveseat. Baba crawls into his cave and lies down, shows me how he sleeps.

Hector goes to request music from the innkeeper and disappears downstairs. I know he's had success when the song switches to Manu Chao.

Over the pass, we drink before bed with impunity. No more midnight sandals on icy flagstones.

All morning: *Om mani padme hum.* And this morning, while walking the main street seeking toilet paper (such a subcontinental noob!), there was Baba on his way up to the temple complex, bent over in the cold, coughing. We talked for a minute—he was with a chubby programmer from Bangalore, bundled in a Shiva-orange North Face, who plans to spend thirteen days in a cave, meditating alone. Baba said he showed him a few caves yesterday (like a real estate agent?) until he decided on a good one, close to the stream.

People at the hotel are talking about flying back to Pokhara, and I say: Hell no.

Bob Marley Hotel is the Goa of the trek after a grueling beginning, uphill all the way, and now we can chill. The start of southbound, of something new. It's a trip back to Baba Lodge, music and motorbikes, pool tables and dreadlocks. And in a way, a downer as well. *This is it?*

I don't want to feel like the trek's almost over. Might need to ask Uncle Sam for an advance on the stimulus package.

The Upstate Oatmeal Eaters' Association: We pack big bowls.

How'd you sleep? Like I'd died from useless small talk. Had a dream no one ever asked me that again. By putting my head on the pillow and closing my eyes.

And in our room—no!—a Western crapper. I'll squat on the seat.

And the mantra means *Hail to the jewel in the lotus*, or a thousand other things.

Jomsom: Blown to Shore

Walked through four hours of wind today from Muktinath to Jomsom, wind tearing down the valley. A 600 meter descent, rocks almost the whole way, brown scrub mountains, and the occasional herd of goats defying gravity. The wind obscured all other sound. Flapped the bill of my hat up or down depending on the angle of my forehead. Twice the hat flew off, but was caught by the neck cord like a dragster parachute. Hector was somewhere far ahead; he's faster on the downhills. After lunch, a flat walk along the riverbed to Jomsom, staring at the ground, one step after the other, click clack click clack with the two sticks, one metal, one bamboo.

Finally reached town, Jomsom, and it's a big (in quotes) town, the type of place you can burn a backup DVD of your photos. I was beat-up by the wind and wanted to throw my stuff down and be done. We made our obligatory stop at two checkpoints, the police and the Conservation Area office, proving we're still alive. The ATM is out of service until 9 a.m. tomorrow—damn!—but I'm not leaving this town until I use it. Splurged at the internet café, 300 rupees to let everyone back home know we made it over the pass.

When you see a broken bottle, ask: How'd the bottle break?

Now I wait for my DVD to finish. Still in full trekking clothes with boots and a knee brace, but an appointment with the shower approaches. Yes, we have a shower in our room. And a Western-style commode. Nuff said. Sometimes I rip on Hector for always picking the top-shelf option, but the shower will be welcome. Nilgiri above us is so snowy it's like something I'd want to eat with coffee.

He sits and waits. He sits and waits for his dinner. Hears the fingerlicking slurping spearing clinking *ahhs* of the couple underway. They talk finances. Prosciutto smuggling, how I made my first million. Rupees. Blew out my knee in the process. But thank God for the massage I got out of it. What was his name? The man who pointed out the door. *Cops!* And the 4-to-1 ratio of rubbers to rubbees, jumbled, jumping onto the fire escape. To climb to the floor above and continue the hijinks. Someone suggested I shave my beard. Advice from a torso's length above. Not when I'm paying. Lumberjacks, Sikhs, Rasputins. Could you resist an army of Rasputins? Could anyone? Riding over the rim of the valley, blade in one hand and touch to stop the bleeding in the other. Could apply it to my checking account. Nepal ain't cheap when you live on yak beef and custard. Bit o' nutmeg on top. The custard plain, midway across Iowa and dropping in value since I sold my plot. They call it the dustbowl now. Bowls and belts, the top bar in Amsterdam. And you thought it was The Cockring. And that's why you have the doctor on Tuesday. No health insurance is a bad place to be in, has you working five 12-hour shifts a week at the junk mail factory. Off the Thruway, got the job offer from a billboard. And you'll get the job swiped out from under you, precisely extracted from your grasp as soon as the robots show up. Cause everyone wants a neat stack. I settle for a neat 'stache. Clean edges. No robots near my face, though, not even an electric toothbrush. Ever seen Terminator 2? Terminator, too? The telephone company bites your balls off. Nothing new. Not like time travel. Which I should have invested in before it took off. Like a Louisiana high school quarterback with a bulging belly of a girlfriend. A nightmare, because you ate chocolate before bed. Bed before chocolate, nothing wrong with that. And chocolate in bed? Optimal. Keep a bottle of syrup on the nightstand. In the guestroom. On Thanksgiving. "Are you trying to tell us you want a sibling?" Nope, the whole hog inheritance works for me. Am I throwing in the towel? What do you mean by throwing? The only two places I'm doing anything in a towel are Arkansas massage parlors and the Fieldcrest proving grounds. Both enterprises indebted to Walmart, of course. Yes, remember the first sales trip to Bentonville. Bent-one-ville more like it. The leverage they apply! You'll be running back to Upstate for a bowl of oatmeal, maybe some pancakes. Cause the syrup ain't the same in the south.

Tukche: Roof of the World

Another day of oat porridge. We're at the Jomsom airport, heading south. But not by plane. We expect to see flights approaching the airport the rest of the way down the valley. Hector's guidebook says the winds will continue for a few days, and I struggle to imagine getting used to it. A surplus of Hindu pilgrims in this town. Mostly old. Thinking about death, thinking about salvation. *Mukti*. Speaking of which—the lodges. What a difference on this side! The *Thakali* rumors are true. Today was my first "Good morning!" from an innkeeper. I don't trust comparisons, but here the wind doesn't get in the room. The food is urbane. There's hot water. More phones per capita. Locals are somewhere else, the workers are professionals from Kathmandu. And again, the food! Yes, this is a more hospitable area, it has an airport and a road—but maybe those came because of the people. Ready to accept the outside world. To trade with it.

And now we're hotboxing the rooftop sunroom at 4:29 p.m. on a Wednesday, as the workday's cranking up back home. I'm glad I don't always feel like the youngest person anymore. And Hector says, "Might as well do like the locals," and tips back the bottle of Tukche Apple Brandy.

What a comfy room we have—a little rooftop cabin with a bathroom, two small beds, all clean wood, and views to the north, south, and east. Our daily laundry line hanging across. Simple. The rooftop sunroom is only a few feet away with booming views of Nilgiri and the Dhaulagiris.

Tea time is out of the budget. Not the worst thing—you can easily fatten up on the trek. On board in the pack: Two Kurkures, four Anand biscuits, one Coconut Creme, one dried apple, and one bottle of apple brandy. The big bottle.

Lodge owners: Send your servants home, hunker down through the dead of winter.

We crossed the pass in bad weather, wrapped in cloud. That counts for something, right? We were surrounded by porters, the back of the pack. The guidebook made me expect the climb to be frustrating, with endless false tops. It wasn't. We were acclimatized and mentally prepared.

When you say *Hajmola?* you say: Sea salt, sugar, black salt, pure whurduk, lemon essence, jeera, black pepper, sunti, and pipalee?

The menu's corner says *Approved, 2000.* No inflation. Someone was here in 2000 paying 200 for a dal bhat.

The apple brandy claims it's 40% alcohol. 80 proof!

Are you walking away from something or toward it? Invent: Bust-a-Nut Nut Butters. Sign of a good hotel: You can perpetually charge to the room. You can charge limos. The minibar—the minibar is the beginning, but the minibar is also the end. My fleece is a gift from a woman who's out there somewhere, lost forever.

A German man, upon finding us sitting in the sunroom with the brandy bottle, a teapot, Kurkure, wafers, dried apples, scattered cigarette filters, a matchbox, Rizlas, a textbook grabbed from the hotel's library as a workbench, and a burning spliff, says, "I hope you're not trying to learn Japanese."

Ad agencies claim to offer the edgiest corporate jobs. Sure, you can rock your tattoos and your weirdness, but it's edgier to fuck someone over to their face.

A good ice shanty is a sunroom. And the bottle of apple brandy is gone. The innkeeper says, "Finished?" And Hector says, "Yes—excellent. And for dessert, could I please have one cup of hot chocolate and the Maceo Parker version of *Tell Me Something Good?*"

Dal bhat and brandy put you over the edge. Chill. The apple brandy is getting stronger in the blood, a slow-release capsule. Or is it my fatigue? Or the hash?

Fox Valley Park: Ball fields, tennis courts, woods surrounding. Trails for bikes or hikes, a pay phone for prank calls, a back route to the elementary school. Softball, soccer, skin your knee, get ticks, crawl through culverts, cross log bridges (you can tell by the construction which kid built each one), add yours, sneak around, climb piles of gravel, *let's go to Fox Valley*, deer in the middle of it, a schizophrenic father's blanket and pile of mail, sunset, bike home, Town of Lewisboro, Residents Only.

Ghasa: Leaf Peeping

A late morning today because yesterday was Brandy Day. Tukche's Famous. No worries. I'll take the extra two hours of sleep for my legs. Despite the alcohol, I remembered to Voltarenize before bed. Spread the smelly muscle cream. Who knows how far we'll walk—the guess is three hours, but if we go through a cooled, clouded afternoon, maybe six. Our budget has reduced us to small pots of tea for breakfast instead of large, and no more mid-afternoon mediums. Though yesterday we ordered a few small pots of hot water. For the brandy. I eagerly await the first peanut butter of the trek, to be delivered with my chapati. Yeah, yeah, yeah, yeah, yeah. Focus.

Walked down from Tukche to Ghasa today. A solid five hours. Good to be back at it. A nice big day, unsure of the kilometer count. Slight headache, possible dehydration. Tonight is our fifth night over the pass. Soon a week. Tomorrow we sleep at only 1,800 meters or so. Getting hotter, but I like the heat. Like sweating. Like showering it off at the end of the day. It seems we're the only ones in this guest house. The Kali Gandaki valley. Let's call it a gorge. The water station's logbook says the group we lost at the pass went through Lete two days ago. Maybe they stayed there and filled their water in the morning. Either way, they're hauling ass. And my beard holds a lot of water. Today we scrambled down a landslide slope in pursuit of wild reefer. Big swaying plants below. Grabbed a couple ounces of leafer and a smaller bit of tippy tops. Not exactly buds, but they might work. Drying now on the sill of our window.

Come here to learn how to live in remote places. A water source, a solar shower, a garden, solar panels. A wood pile. In the kitchen, grinding the dal…

Today, at a crossroads, Hector didn't want to descend. He wanted to spend time at altitude. But the trail went down, and we're following the trail. So down we went. Ate two boiled eggs. Yes, I want a medal. Did I mention the yak steak in Muktinath? Tough, it took an hour to eat. But yak.

The hotel has a picture of the recently deposed King of Nepal on the wall. Like a business with a Bush portrait? It appears we're out of long john territory—for a couple days, at least. We reminisce of a killer fart released in the high camp bedroom right before bed. The ripper wailed in pain and said, "What did I do to deserve this? What did YOU do to deserve this?"

Now standing on the verge of getting it on with the dal bhat. The smells are sweeping stronger, the sizzling continues, and the metallic clanks are diversifying, speeding up.

Sing it like Car 54: *Upstate New York, where are you?*

I almost fall over beneath a craving for Wawa Cookies and Cream ice cream on my dad's couch around 8 p.m. with a cup of coffee to fuel movies until 3:30 or 4.

Mantra: *Thukpa, thukpa, gya-thukpa…*

When you're used to diners, it's hard to feel full after any foreign breakfast. And how can you eat slowly in the morning? I inhale food, vacuum it, offer it asylum, corral it, herd it, shovel it in, deforest my salads and annihilate my plates, lay on, charge, go over the top. If spoons are planes, mine is a dive bomber in reverse, but still leaving nothing behind.

There's that fucker, there in the distance, soon to disappear.

When we get back to Pokhara, I'll turn the walking stick into a pipe to say I smoked out of my stave. For credentials in Vermont.

Hector recalls his last hour in Utica: "After all the packing was done, the apartment was clean, I'm waiting for the inspection to get my deposit, I grabbed the last Saranac out of the fridge and chugged it in the middle of the room." This was two days after the send-off party with all the co-workers he left behind. "I have a picture of myself squirting a gin bucket baster in Deb's face, and Chad's shirt was all wet, and everybody was *wasted*, and Chad and Deb boned on my bed, which was weird because they were both my bosses and both married to other people, and later that night I did Jen on the same bed. While RJ and Natedogg were passed out on the floor of the front room. Then we woke up, Jen disappeared, we blazed, got breakfast, and went to the Saranac brewery, and RJ got a 24-pack of Pumpkin Ale he carried back to White Plains on the Amtrak."

What have you done with some of your family you can't tell the rest of your family?

Be an innkeeper, set up a space for guests: consider the ambience, the surroundings, fit it to where it stands, go for alternative appeal, eco-tech, basic shelter, only logs, a lean-to, a teepee, a shanty. Have a fuel source, a kitchen with a stove, an outhouse/bath/latrine. Consider mobility: the pre-fab trailer on one side, the historic landmark on the other. Have a view—or seclusion. Or both. What it keeps you out of, what it puts you into, what options it provides. Know your maximum (comfortable) capacity, have an overflow area (*you can always crash on the haystack*), have accessibility or lack thereof. A garden. Car parking or none. Rely on feet, snowmobiles, helicopter. How does it look on paper—does it have map appeal? Will topography alone attract interest, cause strangers to stumble on it? Kerosene lanterns, a gas fridge? A shower? Which brings us to the toilet, the deal breaker for many. There has to be an agreeable option. (The pizza man attempts to make a million dollars...)

Hector is a fast walker, and I worry why he walks fast. How often do people tell you, "You're overanalyzing things?"

Weed in the woods. How is it treated differently by the Scouts and by Outdoor Education? Outdoor Ed says *No—but maybe on a rainy day.* Which turns into a blizzard. In which everyone gets hypothermia. In July. And gets saved by a group of Boy Scouts. The same Scouts who, two days prior while overtaking the group, sold the bag of grass for an honest price.

I buy cigarettes from a five year-old. And the British woman says to the boy, "Excuse me, do you have curd? Is it made from proper milk? Can I taste it?"

Ghorepani: Machinations of the Book Broker

Day 20: Fueling up for a seven-hour climb with apple porridge and mint tea. Five thousand vertical feet, the biggest climb yet. Refilled the tea pot from my water bottle. Looking for cheap flavor.

We boomed it up the 5,000 foot climb (just over 1,500 meters), out at 7:15 before the heat, but not for long. Soon we were drenched in the humidity and climbing steeply. Stopped for cookies after two hours, lunch after two more, and continued slowly with hot sauce bellies. We fell in with a group of porters heading into the what the guidebook calls a DANGER ZONE rife with muggers and gropers, and flew up-mountain with them at a finishing-kick pace for the last three hours. Fifteen minutes from the top, monsoon rain hit and we all ducked into a tea house to suit up. The porters wear ponchos, too. The last fifteen minutes was the steepest part of the day. Banged it out. After winding past chortens, we pulled out a map of the town and squinted at it all the way to the lodge. The Super View is at the top of a hilltop development, a circle of lodges ringing a small peak, with northern and eastern exposure toward ALL

THE MOUNTAINS. The lodge's footprint has a bit of a twist, so our room gets cuts of afternoon sun.

Nice town. 2,874 meters, built on the path over a small pass, and expanding in both directions up the saddle for the views. We've chosen the Super View Lodge because how can you argue with their name? And here's the definitive afternoon sunset sunroom.

Hit the secondhand bookshop with *Leaves of Grass*, and traded for something that might become a gift. *Pike*. A book to read before a week in Maine. We'll see. The owner only wanted to give me 100 rupees for *Leaves of Grass*, and *Pike* cost 120. I tried to convince her she could sell it for 250, easy, within a week. Put it face-out in the front window and you'll see. Landmark American work. Longer than any book in here—*Look* (fanning the pages), *poetry. You never finish it!* And in the end, it worked, though her frustration may have sealed the deal. I left with a book weighing a few ounces more than the one I dropped off, which I'm sure will keep her up at night. Until the Whitman sells.

Bought supplies for the Annapurna Sanctuary *after* the book deal—can't show any sign of resources while bargaining. With *Pike* in my vest's inside pocket, picked up muesli, two Coconut Cremes, one Snickers, and stuff for Hector. The secret is to find the foodstuffs not on display, the boxes of plastic bags with scraps of papers inside as labels, printed only in Nepali. That's where the muesli was hanging out. Declined the impending plastic bag and piled it all in my hat. The grocery man liked this, and not only because it raised his profit margin.

Back to Super View, backtracking as best as the chortens allowed. Paused to ask two women where the vegetable guy had gone, the door-to-door salesman I'd passed while descending. He was last seen climbing the stairs into our development with a balance scale of produce over his shoulder. One woman said up, and the pursuit began. Joined up with a British woman who was also seeking produce, and we ascended, crossed a construction zone, and then descended to find him in the courtyard of the lodge below. He didn't respond to her English inquiries, and she didn't respond to the catcalls from the scaffold above us (not even to "two hundred rupees!"), and we almost lost him. My 'O dai!' finally turned his head, and he dropped his load and waited for us to catch up. I think she paid 95 rupees for a handful of things. I gave him five rupees for four chilies, one rupee above fair market value as a formality. I'm content to stand by and watch other trekkers get ripped off for both the benefit of seller, and because I know I'll get a commission in the form of a discount by not helping the others get a better price.

Super View Lodge is super, if you can deal with the hovering staff. Hustling you to eat dal bhat, to eat dinner early (and go to bed), and to do and avoid countless other actions. An exclamation with the enthusiasm of indie rock from the Korean woman in the room next door. Baseball hats in attendance: Orlando Magic, Chicago Bulls, New York, NYC, the Michigan "M" (on the ground, in the dust), *Hauser*. Took a crap while taking a hot shower. Smoked a cigarette in the shower—incense?— upping the ante on smoking in the bath.

Note: Get aspirin before heading to the Annapurna Sanctuary. You don't want to be like a boss asking everyone if they have any. If you get rain two days in a row, try to wash some things.

Chuile: The Adventures of Shitheel von Slipslider

Caught off-guard below Tadapani: We were five or six hours into a day of climbing up and down jungle ravines, steeper than yesterday, fearing muggers, our stashes stashed and scattered around our packs, dodging leeches, passing local kids bleeding from the ankles. We made Tadapani for a noon lunch. Raindrops started when we left, and we soon descended into clouds. Threw on the ponchos and pack covers, and for fifteen minutes it seemed like a false alarm with on-and-off sundrops. But then the drops got bigger and whiter, each drop a perfect sphere of whitewater with a footlong tapering tail. We arrived at a clearing, the top of a staircase of terraces stepping who knows how far down. Ducked into a shed with a chained and down-on-its-luck dog. He didn't move or make a sound while we waited on the rain. After double-checking the map, we headed out down a clay stream-slop through open fields with horses, we ran across the wet grass, and going too fast at the bottom of a not-so-steep slope, I planted my left boot in a meringue of manure, went back on my heel, and on only the heel slid five feet like a roller skating trick, and regained control just before banging shin-first into a wooden gate. Squeezed between its impassable beams and a wall of earth where many had squeezed before, streaking my backpack on the vertical scoop-out of mud, eroding it for the next traveler. By now the heavy rain had returned and we ducked under the balcony of a large, shipshape lodge with a big ol' front yard to wait again. And the rain stayed strong, and was worse thirty minutes later, with thunder heckling the valley from every seat in the terraced theater, and we sat and considered the clouds stacked all the way down to our destination. We agreed the trail would be nasty to continue, even if the rain stopped now, and we parked for the night. So this is the monsoon. People say it's early. Global warming? What if our trip coincides with the headline *Nepal Hit by Worst Monsoon in History*? All of this water, jostling the soil. The land can slide out from under the bed at any time…

Everyone is down with the coconut biscuits. Baseball hats again: Who knew Nepal has so many Yankees fans? Serious stuff: Any corporation that sends you to Manhattan for training. Who knew: The Netherlands used to be Belgium and Holland, but Belgium separated and Holland kept The Netherlands name. Warning: I don't feel full, ever! The night before the flight I will eat: brain curry at United Coffee House in Delhi.

A smiley hip Nepali couple runs the Mountain Discovery Lodge. Are they the off-season caretakers? Their two year-old is bundled up and plopped beside the dining room's wood stove. They're in the kitchen together, hollering, singing, laughing.

An old Nepali woman comes out of the back wearing a burlap sack over her head, cut down one of its two long seams, point up. A cone-topped cape. To her, how does the international Gore-Tex'd crowd appear?

We go up and over ridges, down one and up the next, up one, and down the other side. Each one is an hour down, an hour up. We're building a rhythm of ridges. There's usually a new view on the other side. We walked the ridges this morning (after dragging ourselves to Poon Hill at 4:30 a.m. for sunrise on Dhaulagiri). We left Ghorepani on a side trail, perpendicular to the main road, through the storied dangerous rhododendron forest, and made a quick climb to the top of the ridge. Then a hard left, which pointed us east toward Chomrong by way of Deurali. After another brief climb, we descended to Deurali, continued horizontally along the mountainside, descended to another town, climbed a steep surprise, another up-down. *How'd the river get all the way down there? Didn't realize we were this high...* Descended to the river with a team of porters, the same ones we walked with yesterday. They blew past us, whistling in their sandals, across the actual and angry river, Bhurungdi Khola. (What we'd seen from above was only a tributary). Up for 90 minutes to the aforementioned Tadapani. Another ridgetop, a huge new view. Almost into the Annapurna Sanctuary. *See the village far below? We go there, then left up the valley behind the ridge. Three to four hours. Nice.* Fifteen minutes into the plan, I put on my poncho. And what happened next you've already heard.

I drink hot water with sugar. The Free Tea. Might have to up the tea at home. Green, for caffeine. But it's not as available, and I'll be filling up with gas station drip before I know it. Coffee: I miss the superhuman things it makes me do. People offer stats of their cup per day consumption. But a pizza guy always takes the prize for cups of coffee per shift. I've passed 15 before, but those are little Styrofoam eight-ouncers. It's always there in the delivery station, ready, and if it's not, you're scrambling to make more or calling in a favor.

Innkeepers: Do you bring out the candles? I ask because we've lost power. But landslides are what's scary. Like the one across the valley. It starts at our elevation and rips across the terraces. All the way, all the way down.

Chomrong: Loads of Loads

Breakfast. The Koreans have settled their bill after fifteen minutes of deliberation, and they're out the door, having cleared out the oatmeal supply. No oatmeal! I will restrain myself from stretching the budget to 140 for two pancakes, and instead adjust downward to 70 for one pancake. We're only walking two hours today, so I should be good on fuel.

We're stretching our budget like taffy to get up to the Annapurna Sanctuary and back. I'll need to flee Pokhara upon return, before irreparable damage is done. That's the thing about traveling with Hector—with all of our talking and keeping up and egging on, I haven't mentally reset like I would have if I were alone.

And we're back to eating the mix. We have a freezer bag of the Ghorepani muesli—good stuff, and fresh—and the remnants of the last mix, granola dust and a couple raisins. I spend ten minutes dicing and crumpling a Snickers bar into the bag, mostly well distributed, but still some handfuls are more lucrative than others. The mix could use a day in the pack for the chocolate to melt and disperse. We keep an eye out for stuff to toss in, you know the feeling, *I could throw it in the mix.* And all of a sudden you're spooning the breakfast table's granulated sugar into the bag.

Crumpling hash is like making the mix. Would you expect anything else? We'll trade our sunscreen for your Iodine pills—too late, found another taker. The Himalayan barter economy. Do you have this thing in your brain where, upon meeting certain people, a flag goes up: *Remember the name!*

A banging on the door of our room, and we open it to find a German couple. And the man says, all slow and superior, "Would you mind taking your load elsewhere?"

Load? I say, "Our laundry?" It prayer-flags across the room on two tightropes of twine.

"Your smoke," he says, and his wife hits an imaginary roach.

"Oh. Yeah, no problem. Didn't mean to bother you."

"We have children next door." They leave and close the door.

And Hector says, "What's with these people? They should know better—this is not a family atmosphere." The load stays where it is, arranged on the sill like a flowerbox, drying in easy reach. Though we switch to smoking it at the end of the balcony, sharing with the innkeeper.

And Hector says, "Machapuchare is so close, I don't have to use my zoom."

We should have offered to light some incense. Would it have helped the situation? No, too much of a connotation. I understand. My parents were none too pleased when I started burning it in my room in seventh grade. Not against it, per se, but curious as to What's Going On Up There. Not smoking, of course. Just the vibe, one step closer to the Shangri-La the health class warns of—especially when combined with Christmas lights. Their rainbow twinkle was visible through the curtains, making the neighbors wonder what the two girls from up the street—who went in the front door an hour ago—are doing underneath them. Nothing more than standing over the tip of the burning incense, inhaling it, and upon visual confirmation of an exhaled cloud, whispering, "We're smoking!"

Hector points out the back window of our room and says, "Look at this guy! He's cutting down the weed plants!" And sure enough, a guy with a big curved knife is hacking down not only the wild weed, but every plant and putting it all in a bucket. I propose he knows we're smoking it, so he's preemptively harvesting. "No, dude," Hector says. "He's going to feed it to animals." And how it is: All you need is a big curved knife.

The storms are stronger up here. We're closer to Annapurna I, the storm producer. We walked over three ridges today, a direct stomp from our emergency pull-off the night before.

Long johns under a pair of pants: We all know the trouble they bring. When you're burning more calories than you're taking in, do you drop less deuce? My guess: Yes.

Considerations for the ideal dal bhat experience: The seat where it's easiest to get a refill. A yellow papad, salted, verging on tortilla. Soybean nuggets taste like chicken. Any type of pickle (in Nepal, you pickle whatever's around). The obligatory deep-dish steel plate. Dal juice flooding its segments. Spoonfuls straight from the cookpot for the refills, something green, hopefully with vitamins. Mystery mushrooms.

Tonight I'll stick with two servings, it's as much food as if I ate three. Not pushing the third refill—already fearing intestinal retribution for what I've consumed, all the way down to the sugar cabbage, both onions (found you under there), though not all of the salad, nor all of the beany pickle.

Hector, staring at the summit of Machapuchare, says, "What do you feel when you look up there?"

"It'd be pretty damn hard to deliver a pizza to the top."

And who delivered the first pizza to the summit of Everest? Has it been done? The Tenzing Norgay of pizza. Who will claim the honor?

The innkeeper's wife gazes at the trekkers across the courtyard, not us. Can't blame her, they're more likely to place an order.

To the man with a porter and clean sneakers: Excuse me, can I take a picture of your Esprits? How are your shoes so white? Shoes shouldn't be so white in this part of the world. How do you keep them so? On a Nepali's back? I hope you pay well for the privilege.

When trouble hits: *Excuse us, we're on government duty.*

A cloud rolls up the valley, smitten with Annapurna, first a tentacle, a finger approaching from around the bend, opaque white (like the shoes), then another, bigger, curling, goosing, now rolling around us and flooding the valley until all we see is Kalpana Guest House fifty meters below. And now it's blocked.

…and that was a Vermont gas station deuce. Hector has the hardcore Indian gastrointestinal tract. Coming from the States, it's like I'm working with an old version of Windows.

When you bring your children to Nepal, your children will learn what burning marijuana smells like. You can tack on any lecture you choose. This is my hotel room. My house, for tonight.

In a storm with bunkmates, rip ass like Shawshank: Time 'em with the thunder so nobody wakes.

Do not despair, for the hungry shall be called to the table. I say beautiful when the oatmeal arrives like I'm qualified to use the word.

And Hector says, "If you can get it for 15, get me one." We've been reduced to bargaining for ramen in rupees, putting limit orders on dry noodles. But hey—the local flavor forces us to eat despite our budget. How do you ration a big bag of snacks? A big bag of anything?

Himalaya Hotel

Out at 7 a.m., descended half an hour of stairs, stocked up on aspirin and chocolate at the base. Then over the bridge and up the ridge we'd seen the previous day, around the corner, and into the sanctuary. Wet green forest, mud, stones, and drips. Gnarly, smelling like the Northeast, but overrun with bamboo. We made Bamboo (the town) quickly, pepped along by a dog we call Snickers. An hour to the next town, lunched, and said *why not*, and walked another hour up the mountain to Himalaya, the ascent we'd dreaded yesterday.

I sing a lot of Cypress Hill around here. Emphasis on crops.

Cesar from Brazil sneers at our tola nub and dubs it The Black Shit. Primary definition, no slang usage. Pronounced *sheet*.

How to crank an appetite to the max: Hikes, hash, and Hajmola. Poster on the restaurant wall: Neither a borrower nor a lender befriend, for a loan loses both itself and friend. Did you know Bhutan makes great jam? Do you know how the Hindu version of heaven differs from the Christian? You do business in Bangalore? Big whoop. The porters sleep behind the outhouse, and that ain't cool.

Hector reminisces on an early camping experience: "I had the zipper to the top of the sleeping bag, and at 3:30 a.m., in the dark, the puke just came…"

Annapurna Base Camp

In the middle of the night, the lodge started shaking, and I knew this was it, the landslide, and I yelled *Hector! Hector!* And then I realized nothing was shaking, it was a dream. And so I went back to sleep, to a gigantic frat house where I played the central role in an Oedipus triangle, but not with my actual mom and dad, but with stock characters, and yes, I killed the dad, got blood stains everywhere, and didn't go to school, knowing the police would soon arrive with questions. I accepted the fate of suicide. Then I bedded the platinum wife (fine, mother), and enjoyed a follow-up from her old-enough daughter (don't ask me how it works). I applied a mental brake to avoid a mess. I boarded up the frat house in a rush, draping chain mail behind the windows and nailing heavy slabs in front. We left. Today at breakfast, the innkeeper asks if we felt the earthquake. He says they get them all the time.

We follow the river to the lap of Annapurna, work with the weather, rush to beat the rain. We are trekking in the monsoon—in the middle of last night I woke up with the room shaking. A confirmed earthquake. So the mountains throw surprises. We gun it through avalanche zones like yellow lights. The innkeeper says, "Way up there is a massive amount of snow." We climb over mossy rubble in the woods, where a truck-sized boulder teeters on the edge of a cliff. We walk beneath its belly. We cross slimy river rocks and think *big rapids down there.* The Belgian man thinks we hike too fast. He says, "You guys are going like pirates!" Maybe we are. Like a Pittsburgh pitcher on the twelfth of June in 1970.

Cesar the Brazilian coffee farmer traded a grow room for a purebred Border Collie, male. Cesar of the three big balls. Of charas. Cesar is making the commitment to home and work. Going home. Hector is stapling himself to graduate school. And me? All I want is to be rolling on wheels.

ABC, easy as 1, 2, 3—yes, I've had Jackson 5 in my head for the past two days. We made it to Annapurna Base Camp, the Sanctuary, barely beating the rain. We take a stone room in the lodge.

A big stomping woman mixes a Khukri rum and Coke. And I want to make oatmeal in Madison County. But here, immediately upon arrival, I may have gone too far by ripping the one-footed pants-off fart while changing into long johns. We only have so much incense left.

Do you know what real mountaineering boots look like? Do you know who Tomaž Humar is? When was the last time you had hot chocolate with pizza?

We are all about to die. An open flame kerosene burner has been ignited beneath the lodge's dining room table. The innkeeper says, "Now we lock it in..." And like pallbearers we scoot the wooden bench closer to table and tuck in the heat-trap blanket.

After half of a small cheese pizza, I miss the streets of pizza more than ever. Italian food—Oliveri's, Portofino, Nina's, Cavallo's—I want to walk into Oliveri's and demolish. It was gone too fast, I wish I had the wing basket to pick from, a fresh slice pie coming out, even a PowerAde. WINGS. Wings and baseball. One can of beer is left in the lodge's display case, my god, it's like an unplugged Utica fridge.

In our whitewashed stone and plaster room at Annapurna Base Camp, mid-day, I try to keep warm in my sleeping bag under a blanket, wearing a bandanna, wool hat, puffy vest, fleece pull-over, nylon t-shirt, long undershirt, long johns, cloth cotton pants, shorts over the pants, nylon sock liners, and thin wool socks. I'm considering mittens. My feet are nearly numb. I have pair of SmartWool socks drying. They'll keep me warm, but I don't want their dampness on my feet. Maybe I can smuggle a pair under the table at dinner to dry for bedtime. No chance of a new pair until tomorrow morning, it seems.

The muesli gas is out of control, something's about to break. My schema of highway rest stops: an initial fork, cars one way, trucks and buses another, pull into the car lot where wandering people weave through the cars clutching paper bags of greasefood and big cups, a conversion van lurches in reverse and almost hits you, there's a map board, a chart of driving times, tourism pamphlets for places you'll never go, direct-to-the-hotel phones, a high-traffic bathroom with a wet floor sign. At the food stalls, confusion over who's in line for which counter, a sticky unpredictable ketchup pump. There's calculation of the ETA, maybe some gas or rudimentary maintenance, there's a flagpole and a cop, dog walkers, and maybe you run through the rain. Playing the market (*where's the cheapest coffee?*), vending machine temptations, arranging the food in the car for easy driver consumption, backing out with utmost caution, moving forward, putting on shades, using all of second and third gears, back in the race.

When was the last time you sang *Kum Ba Yah*?

Tomorrow we rest, and then things change. We start walking back. The walk's not over, no, only walking back toward Pokhara. Maybe three or four days. Rock out two nights in the Poke. Then Kathmandu. Oh boy. Nothing I like better than checking the clock and seeing it's half an hour till dal bhat.

You want poetry? Try sour plum Hajmola. You're either always up for hot chocolate or you're not. You've got a golf ball of hash? Hit it with a nine iron.

The innkeeper tacks on a charge for the dining room's heater: The club's cover. Whether you like it or not, if you stay here, you're chipping in for fuel.

The Ridges: Like walking the length of a Toblerone. The back of a stegosaurus. I find myself giving advice: "The forest from Chomrong to Ghorepani is soaking. Lot of leeches."

A mountaineer is dying on Annapurna. Cesar cups the candle and says, "This candle is his life." Cesar who in Thailand drank seven mushroom shakes and lost two pairs of flip flops in a night. Cesar who tells a Belgian to his face Twix is the world's best chocolate. Cesar who says, "Yeah, I heard these cooks, if they don't like you, they put their hands up their ass." Cesar who says of the Belgian, "He's the kind of guy, I think they kill him if he goes to Pakistan. They say, 'What man, you don't like my toilet?' And they kill him."

The propane in the dining room is thick, choking. I don't trust this gas smell. I leave to bask in my own. It's moonrise in the sanctuary. The only thing that can make the mountains look small.

Air Traffic

Cesar says to the portrait artist, "Come on, what a big nose is this?" But she's drawing me, not him. I rock the schnozzola with pride, the good ol' Neapolitan honker. I tell her to put in extra hair, dandruff in the beard, maybe some eyebrow flakes, a trans-nostril snot ring, chapped lips, and dal bhat debris.

Think about the cost of a month, wherever you are.

We woke today at 4:45 a.m. to find the Sanctuary clear of clouds, the ten mountains around us like the view you don't want of the volcano. We climbed a ridge sewn with prayer flags and took nonstop pictures, enduring the cold without gloves for a sideshow-feat hour and a half. Then down to bed—wait, no—the sun's out and it's *warm*? Back up into the boulders to lounge for another hour, mugging with our beards clamped between our teeth, hair greased into punk spikes, then down for oat porridge and hot cocoa, pouring some of the cocoa in the porridge like true Americans. Then out front, to the other side of the lodge to watch clouds creep up the valley and engulf us. Ann from Belgium drew my portrait (looking quite Ted Kaczynski these days) and then it was cold again, about to rain, so into the sleeping bag for a three-hour nap until 1 p.m. And yes, I downed the whole cheese pizza, unsure whether it was yak or powdered mozzarella (leaning towards latter), and it brought back all of the days my fridge had a box wedged above the crisper drawers where a shelf would have been, doing the job of a shelf, holding a leftover any-type pizza to be reheated in the toaster oven as often as the conscience allowed. I miss a strong cold upstate morning deuce, the sort of dashing-for-the-border stink smuggler chased out of town by four perfect slices of wheat toast with strawberry jam and Steely Dan. This isn't the first time my days have revolved around an early wakeup.

Enjoy the mornings. At 2 p.m. the clouds tuck you in for a nap.

Do you live in a place where you need a space heater to shower?

There's an emergency on the mountain, a sick climber stuck at 7,500 meters with cerebral edema has been unconscious for five days. One climber is with him, and another is above, almost at the summit, but now apparently heading down. Swiss climbers left from Base Camp (4,130 meters) yesterday morning to help with the rescue. News came this morning rescuer was sick, one continuing, breaking trail through heavy new snow. We've heard avalanches today.

A helicopter was supposed to come this morning to drop rescue climbers (the sick man's friends) and medicine at 5,000 meters, but the chopper was too small... Around 10 a.m. we heard a chopper approaching through the clouds, but with zero visibility we only heard it come and go. It dropped the climbers and gear at Machapuchare Base Camp, 400 meters downmountain. They ate lunch here and are on their way up. An agitated blonde Canadian in her early 20's, the girlfriend of the sick climber, is orchestrating the rescue. She's using a satellite phone loaned by the big stomping woman, who works for the UN. The big stomping UN woman sits at the lodge's table and drinks Khukri rum and Cokes. She calls one of the rescue climbers "a real ladykiller." She has a low-expectations posture.

In these conditions, with cold monsoon rain and snow falling daily, plus a multi-day rescue schedule, things are grim. Now it's 3 p.m. and we've smoked the day's eighth joint. Time to make another bid at warming the sleeping bag. Even with the bag and a blanket pulled up to my armpits, it's a fifty-fifty chance.

I've given up on goals. Service can shove it, I want hot food, an endoscopy, and a BJ or two. I'll pick up some crazy jeans. Maybe flee the workplace after a week, freak out and bounce. I'll set myself out there as cougar bait, with a dashing hat, a shot of cologne in the crotch, and a trailer. I will go cyclone on junk food, the crunchy shit, the chocolate sticks, the Japanese gels. It's going to be messy.

And Hector says, "If we don't eat anything between lunch and dinner, we can get a pizza." Which would be a fitting way to celebrate my beard's birthday.

Do you find yourself missing the luxury of empty international flights?

When I got this knife as a Cub, I never thought—at all—it would cut blocks of hash in Nepal.

Landmark moment: Discovery of the receding hairline. But none yet in our room, Smoke Lounge #4. We plot to upend the Duty Free Shopping industry with Dirty Free Shopping. And there's something scheming about prowling the supermarket after 8 p.m.

Eleven joints for the day, and now dinner. All afternoon, one room, no light, in bed, smoking the green spirit, sleeping, farting, communicating with grunts. But that's what you do up here. It's an extreme environment, not a Goan bask-in-the-nature kind of place. You have to hold your own against the elements. And this morning, when the conditions were good, we were out there with the glacier glasses, hopping on and off rocks, standing on edges, posing or being possessed. Five and a half hours. A feat of endurance considering things get good at 4:45 a.m. We're not guilty, not ashamed, not feeling like lesser mountaineers—we're not bagging any summits. And now we rest. We pick up the packs again tomorrow.

Old Delhi: Karim's is cream-your-jeans good.

When you have a choice between the mom-and-pop gas station and the fluorescent-lit Citgo, consider: Certain deuces require a corporate environment. Where if someone knocks, you have no shame in stating a non-negotiable *five minutes*. The Ultimate Fudge Brownie sold at a particular gas station near Jeffersonville, Vermont, should be renamed the Bunker Buster.

When you're camping and it's dark, a clean deuce can be dropped within shouting distance of the campsite. A sloppy deuce belongs on the other side of the tracks. Beware the peanut sauce noodles. For any deuce held more than 24 hours, the dropper must file a post-drop Deuce Report.

Do you remember the last time you bought a new t-shirt? Have you been homesick enough to visualize, in real time, making and eating a bowl of cereal? Speaking of gastronomic memories: screw the Alamo, remember the kulchas of Amritsar! It's been a big yawny day. In Chomrong, they're picking rice.

Above 900 meters, 22°C is the ideal temperature to grow coffee. You need rain and sun, and a dry winter for picking.

In India, did you make dal bhat gas? We did. All day, all night. Have you ever found yourself describing every type of Halloween candy available down to Hershey's kisses? Every type of chocolate multiplied by every type of center: peanut butter, milk chocolate, dark chocolate, mint chocolate, almonds, cherries. Green spirit, teen spirit. And this room smells like green spirit. The new release. The upgrade. In Pokhara, you have to pay for the dealer's rounds of pool at Laila's to get a peek at it.

Khukuri cigarettes: Cut your throat.

Here, you get in the sleeping bag, scratch the balls for half an hour, smoke, eat, fart, scratch, repeat. It's the night before we leave the Sanctuary. From here, it only gets hotter. For a long time.

What's the drunkest someone's ever been and flown—without crashing—a helicopter? I want to know the BAC.

The Great Pyramid of Giza is the evolution of the Eifel Tower. What if we're going backwards?

Cesar, regarding the hassle of stepping into Himalayan cold to urinate, says, "In Everest, I take a bottle to the room, one time I pissed 700 mL's, man."

Current mailing address: Room #4, Snowland Lodge, South Annapurna Base Camp, Nepal.

Cesar, regarding the symmetry of his cone, says, "You have to be very smart to roll a joint like this."

We decamp to the dining room. The UN woman has gotten caught in the rain without her poncho. She who pounds Khukri rum while scratching her ass at dawn? Oh yes, all of us here have the funk. She who arrives, loans a phone, and orders all sorts of sugar-filled snacks. She who could shovel the runway at O'Hare.

And Hector says, "I never pay for sex."

And I say, "Yeah, I'm still wrestling with getting the rub and tug, but I can file that under massage."

And the innkeeper says, "Sexy talking makes bad weather."

And Hector says, "We'll talk about deuce. Deuce doesn't offend the gods."

Chances of a Sanctuary sunset, as always, are low to impossible.

And Cesar brandishes a glob of hash the size of a Selectric typewriter ball. And I miss Granada.

A small cheese pizza for myself? Could it be? And my wallet says, "Your hummus days are done."

Final Approach

Leonardo DiNardo! We've stayed another day. And now broken the sound barrier, punched through to the other side: the x or y joint of the day (smoked over lunch in the lodge's dining room) cracked the permastone, and we were reduced to giggling grunting lumbering clods, operating on the cerebral plane of brontosauri. Wormed my way into the sleeping bag and under the blanket, worked up one more cone with the drying-for-two-days leafer, mostly as a farewell (cutting weight for tomorrow morning) and went down, down, down into dreams of beaches.

Now waiting on the evening's dal bhat, taking a chance after this morning's discomfort. I've been hoping for three days the German *take your load elsewhere* family arrives soaked.

And the rescue pilot says, "At 5,600 meters, it's fifty-fifty whether you land or crash. The wind changes a little bit, the weight is off by 20 kilos..." They did everything they could, but the sick climber couldn't swallow the medicine. The rescue pilot tells of an American who was trekking with his girlfriend to Everest Base Camp. He wandered off the trail taking photos, got lost, disappeared. His girlfriend backtracked, found a phone, and called his dad. The dad contacted the embassy, the embassy started a search, and they looked for two days. On the last sweep, the pilot spotted an orange cuff, and the teams below found the American in a crevasse, dead.

The co-pilot says, "He is senior pilot, 17,000 hours. He is from Russia, very famous. Very, very famous." The pilot says India steals all the good pilots from Nepal with four times the pay. He earned good money dropping trekkers at 12,000 meters for the Kailash hike up to 18,000. He dropped a father and son, the dad was 80 years old, the son was 30, and the son got AMS. The pilot evacuated them to Kathmandu. The pair jetted to Singapore and back to the USA, where the son developed complications and, two weeks later, died.

The climber is dead. He tried to climb the South Face of Annapurna. And we've been fighting to get up and take a piss? Please. And for the innkeepers here, things keep going, empty as always. For the first time in a long time I don't want to eat. But I need to keep warm like everyone else, and the cave man urge persists: a couple Coconut Cremes would be good. We stayed an extra day, and maybe the drama was partly why—and now he's dead. We got what we waited for—an ending. We've all read enough Krakauer to know this is what happens in the mountains. Three days under the toe an 8,000 meter mountain—when I tell you I went there, don't assume it was fun. Don't smile and say *Tell me all about it!* Be careful. And consider, before you come here, this place can bring the horror, and you might get stories you don't want to share.

Back to Bamboo

Waiting in the dining room. Cold. Waiting for Hector to get out of bed. We trade places as the one who protests early mornings. What happened to beating the rain? Come on, get up, it's cold as yak balls and cloudy and we have to get back.

And can't you keep it simple, Hector, so we can get out of here? Bastard orders apple pancakes. But at least I'm ready to get soaked today, so no complaining if we're wet before Bamboo. It's been a detached three days up here, and the walk back will be that—back. Same trail, same towns. Get back to Pokhara, then get to Kathmandu and put a vise on the wallet. Yes, food is enchanting up here, but down there with the rain and the heat I'm sure I'll be back to plain ol' street fry. Slow apple pancakes, but I'll do what I can to get out of this with the friendship unscathed.

What are we walking for on the way back? We're on the return leg of the pilgrimage. We've seen death. Damn. You might not get a story you can tell with a smile. Hot chocolate, done. Oatmeal nowhere in sight. Deuce brewing. You and your apple pancakes. The chopper may attempt to fly out in these clouds with the body. A whiff of supermarket bakery. Good rolls. Let me out of this den, let me start testing my knees.

Rolling Out

And hello, welcome to the last day of the hike. Not a lot
happening. You should be moving on. Go get a real breakfast, diner style,
ham slices and nonstop coffee. Drive somewhere. Park, get out, walk.
Maybe bring a book. It's cold here. There too? I assume you have proper
insulation. Me, I'm prairie dogging it in a pair of long johns and thin
cotton pants. Colorful Goan print. Too colorful for heaven. Not colorful
enough for these mountains.

5. Pokhara Again

At Everest Steak House, Cesar proposes to the waitress. The woods change your head. The waiter has his own expertise, he manipulates the lighting control board on a table-by-table basis.

Across the street at Laila's Restaurant and Bar, I find the green spirit for a dollar a gram. And later at the Busy Bee, learn there's no win-by-2 rule on the foosball table

Do you drop *I've been here before* into your conversations?

The Busy Bee's guitar player is SOLID. Is that John Scofield's influence in his solo, or is it what I want to hear? Since return, I forget large chunks of my errands. Yes, my mind is changed. I want to be the fighter pilot who lands and smirks down from the cockpit, gives a cramped thumbs up. Though glacier glasses are an upgrade from aviators.

Travel: Where the only time you say *same old city* is when you're singing along to the cover band. A mosh pit develops. Deep Purple, *Paranoid*. Steppenwolf, *Born to Be Wild*. And I say, "Heavy version." And Hector says, "A heavy virgin?" In the pit you find people with different perceptions of pain.

And the British woman says, "I'm living with seventeen Nepali girls"

And Hector says, "Nuns?"

"No."

"The opposite?"

And an hour or so later, with the Busy Bee near empty, I discover an unflushed, undigested salad in the bowl of the toilet. And Hector says,

"You'd think bulimics are experts at fixing the plumbing." And what do I do? Pile on top of it like federal spending.

I finally see a man wearing a football helmet on a motorcycle.

6. Thamel, Kathmandu

Hector is gone, prowling in Thailand. I don't have the budget to join, so I'm sweating in Thamel. First dream in Kathmandu: I killed Nazis in close combat, used my Swiss Army knife for the jumping jugular surprise, threw trekking poles as spears when my gun was stolen.

So this is where the pizza guy ends up: Notebook nearly empty, naked, trying to drink a beer while lying in bed. 9:30 p.m. From the north, a cover of Candlebox (again), from the west, *Grease*—in Mandarin. Back and forth between isolation and forced smiles. The only people I've seduced in the past few months are merchants. *I live in Costa Rica, give me the sneakers cheap.* I want the morning to come so I can start over. But instead I go out.

Tonight's appetizer: Two Long Island iced teas, served tall and chilled to freeze. You can be in Kathmandu for any reason, from the summit of Everest to the basement of the American Embassy. A solid mix of business and recreation. For dinner: Two more Long Islands. And now to crowd watching. Hookers, hustlers, and helmets. Man crouches eye level with begging children and points at himself, a paper, himself, a paper. A lesson, apparently.

Do you think it's crazy to eat the Kathmandu cocktail's cherry? Do you make brief, weird, and definitively final contact with the street hawkers? Have you ever passed a note to a waiter saying *Where's the funk?*

On me: two biceps bulging from a black t-shirt ending in two hands, one gripping a pad and the other a pen, and every vein between raised like an argument, ready to pop.

The sign above the bar's entrance says Guinness Available. The cover band takes on *Born to be Wild*. Again. I'm back for another Long Island. Top it off with a dollop of French? Yes. Could it be hot wax, like Krakow? Last night in Kathmandu proper—and? Stood up. Nah. What to do about my footstink? Drink it away. Fashionably: something with ice, synthetic to go with the sound of the Rhodes, padded, ivory smooth, creamy, like a cushion you can melt into, a seat you finally don't have to negotiate with. The Smell of Momos. A title? Out to the ashram in Thankot tomorrow after buying a belt and shampoo. *Viva Las Vegas*. Legs and Vegas. TCB! Picked up T.C. Boyle's *Budding Prospects*. Said to myself, "It's not fair to reject a book because it has a pot pun title." It sat on the floor of Ol' Yeller at one point, checked out but never checked into. I was spent after *The Tortilla Curtain*. She sat, reading Dubliners. He sat, feeling Italian in the crotch, waiting for her, till he eventually headed home. With her. For quote-unquote pizza. A slice of Sicilian.

Obama has captured the nomination. Now, no scandal please. You can fall on the stage, sure. But damn, you've come so much further than the Dean Scream. And I'm here, sitting outside the swirling mayhem, and yes, by mayhem I mean people getting hacked to pieces. These yawns have to stop or I'm-a gonna roll another pinner. In the comfort of my room. In the nude. In solitude. And regretful confusion—what happened?

"What'd you do the night Obama locked it up?"

"There was this woman from Quebec..."

Who from here on will live only in fantasy. As obtainable as the BBC weatherwoman. But no sour grapes. My pre-ashram shopping list is growing. Now I have to go two months on a budget stretched thinner than the cheese atop my pizza.

I ask for beard trim at a Thamel beauty salon. But when she starts cutting with plastic kindergarten scissors, I stand up, say *no no no*, give her 50 rupees, and walk out.

The first Sunday of college, I went to the university church because I felt guilty not going. I excused myself from the service and puked hangover sludge in the church basement's sink. In Glasco, I lived in a barn with a rat's nest below it and worms in the carpet. Meditation is like pledge, doing pushups in the basement of your mind. Bag will be packed tomorrow, throw it all in messy. It's only a few miles upmountain.

7. The Kathmandu Retirement Plan: Words from an Elder

The bad trip narrowly avoided: I'm a train, and now I'm a tunnel. I've done acid more than a thousand times. Ask me how's the view. Kids these days, they say the stuff is strong. It's not. It's 50 mics, 100 mics at most. But still, you don't want to be around any jangly vibes. Always have a halfway guy, someone to keep you off the roof. The heaviest hit I took was a thousand mics. Guess that makes a gram. I put on frosted glasses, earplugs, lay on my bed, closed my eyes, and told myself to relax. And with no input, there was no indication at all I was high. First timers? I give them 500 mics. I want to be sure they die.

It's better in the countryside. Acid's vacuum is too strong in the city, strangers get sucked to you for conversation. My buddy had a tabbing machine in his truck, and he had to keep moving. Said he couldn't stay too long in one spot. People flocked from all over, jumping over eight-foot fences. Now, a plain-old sensory deprivation chamber, it's not so much how you feel in there, it's the rush of life when you leave. The complications of a single tree: too much.

In Maui, we started off with the rent paid for three months, with only dope and food, and when the food was gone, we had to figure out something. My buddy and I went downtown, and I had just enough money for a bowl of soup—which we shared—and while we were eating it, a man walked in and said, "You two—I need two guys for my jewelry shop."

We told him about our house, and he came over with a bunch of grinding wheels, a whole setup, and he gave us a big resin ball to eat, and we got to work, grinding chunks of coral into teardrops. He would give us bags of black coral chunks, and we would work and work on the grinding wheels, the whole house, everybody on acid all day, *WHRRRRRRR*. And when we finished them all, I brought them to the guy for the money and he gave me another couple bags of blanks. We became a factory.

One day I found a kilo of grass on the beach, beat-up by the tide, and molded into a fist-size clump. I took it home, put it in the oven, dried it out, and it looked like grass again. But it was compacted, which makes for some strong stuff. Here in Nepal, the hash has the most broken-down, aged cannabinol—which makes the high last—but it's not as strong. It's light and it lasts a long time. In other words, it's smooth. Read Starks' *Marijuana Potency*.

When I was 25, I was in a mad love affair, but everything changed when I moved to from San Francisco to Marin County. Sausalito. I started working as a carpenter. I wasn't smoking then, didn't have any interest at all. Until the guy I was rooming with decided he wanted to try pot. We got some and smoked it in our room. It really hit me—

In '46, I met a German woman who'd used the Nazi soap, the stuff they made from the bodies in the camps, and—I couldn't believe it—she said, "It wasn't any good, it was only for washing clothes."

A man sat next to his sick wife's bed, her head was swollen with cancer. She couldn't talk, couldn't move, and he was talking about her in the past, saying things like, "She was so pretty." And silent tears rolled down her pumpkin face.

I think about my past a lot. I think, "God, what an idiot, why'd you do that!" I kick myself for sleeping with my girlfriend's best friend. A no-no. It blows the whole relationship. You know other places you can get it. You don't have to go to her best friend.

I was on a houseboat party in Sausalito, flirting with this blonde. I got her number, and then this guy started talking to me, talking weird. I didn't know if he was trying to pick me up or her or what. Later I learned his show had debuted that night in Oakland. In one word? Tricky.

On big ships I've had people tell me, "If I get the chance, I'll kill you." Or they say, "If I see you above deck after dark, I'll kill you."

I've been listening to a group from Mozambique. FUNKY. In an Afro-Cuban kind of way. Listen—this chorus is the devil on your shoulder. Complex and sophisticated, but not uptight. Loose and relaxed. Let me show you the disc—how do you open this fucker? There we go— still spinning!

It takes an extra day to heal if you use cold medicine. It's symptomatic relief. Those symptoms make you better. Tea tree oil kills warts. And for poison oak, lacquer thinner. Wet a rag and rub it on the rash, toward the center so it doesn't spread, then toss the rag. It dissolves, the resin breaks down the protein. And athletes foot? Lemon juice. But things can sneak up on you. Out of nowhere, I found a one-inch hair hanging from my earlobe.

Lately I've been searching for good places, at the city level. Antigua, Guatemala, Thailand.

The Army sent me to Germany as a 19 year-old Company commander for 250 Polish guards dressed in U.S. uniforms dyed black. We had ten U.S. non-coms and a German secretary. I was sneaking around one night in the hills above the base, and I rounded a bush and ran right into a guy sticking a submachine gun in my face. A Russian. The guy put his finger to his lips, *shhh,* and we went our separate ways.

I went drinking with twelve Polish officers. Nine drank until they hit the floor, and the other three were still drinking when I left.

I work out on the road. You can lie on your back on the bed and do the breaststroke. Sissy pushups, kneeling on the knuckles. And shadowboxing.

In California, my whole family was in the car, on the coastal highway. My dad lost control, but he pointed the car downhill to avoid rolling it, and he aimed for stumps, hit the one and took it out, aimed for a second and took it out, too. The car caught on the third, and I opened the door and peeked over the side and it was all sheer walls. The whole family could have gone over.

Another time, I jumped for a train and caught it, but my body swung under, and I was hanging over the rails. The wheels almost sliced me in half. But I kept my cool till I was back in the door, and then I started shaking. Then once, doing ninety miles per hour in a Cadillac across Texas, my buddy at the wheel driving for the first time in his life, we got a blowout. We crossed the yellow line three times, and we were lucky, because it was a bridge and we bounced from rail to rail. Anywhere else, it would have been a twenty foot drop into a canal.

The guy on the cargo ship hated me because I was American, no other reason. He'd get drunk and wave a big knife around.

This is my man purse. I don't care. You have plenty of strap-carried things in the army. I used to carry a flute, then a recorder, then a harmonica, and now I whistle. This is Pachelbel's *Canon*—

I got a map of San Francisco and walked up and down every street, and marked each restaurant on my map, and wrote a little review. Made a tourist map called *Gourmet on a Budget*, with a red stripe across the cover, under the title, with white letters: *Eat Out For Less!* They sold like hotcakes. Then I took the cheapest spots and made a separate map for them, called it *Gourmet on a Cheaper Budget*. Did it all up on the typewriter, did all the artwork myself, and took it to a printer. Because you need offset to sell.

I busted up my hearing shooting the rocket gun in basic training. I talk too loud. Had a bottle of buffalo milk on the Pokhara bus until it spilled down the aisle. Play chess all day. I eat a spoonful of butter and honey for breakfast. I'm thinking about heading down to Bangalore to learn about the computer, I need to know how to put my pictures on the internet. I used to chug quarts of half and half. My father ate raw eggs, peanuts with the shells on. I've lost three umbrellas in Nepal. People say I'm losing things because I'm old. I say I've been losing things all my life. It's not getting any worse. I must have lost fifty wool caps. I still say *gee*.

And when I found out about Santa Claus, I said, "I'll never trust an adult again." And never have.

8. Attempted Ashram

I don't know why I'm here. I should have seen this coming, should have checked out other options, don't want to be the smiling foreign dude. I want to make money. I want to smoke cigarettes and die. I'd have to pay ten dollars a day to come and go as I please. Instead, I pay five and teach orphans. So maybe I should take my money home and start over.

I don't want to be won over by the Guru. He's not here. They say he'll be here soon.

Have I been softened up by three months of restaurants and ganja? What if I stay here a month and go home? What are my options? Yes, doctor, I think I'm depressed, coming off a mountainous high.

Took a quick walk into the village and bought a chocolate bar and a back-up pen because I only have one pen. I don't want to go home weakened by this place. Walked past a school I might like to teach in, where I could be an actor and have my role and then leave, and not have to be on 24/7. "Tell me about the teaching you did in Nepal," the phone interviewer will say. "It never happened, I busted out of there in less than a week, no big deal. I needed the visa extension for Annapurna regardless, and—" Head back upstate? Get a room in Bethlehem, PA? Damn—I need cash. And a job. I miss everyone. Hey. Wake up. This is good. I don't want to teach English to anyone but myself.

The ashram uses numbered plates and spoons. And when I ask the kid, "Is that your room?" he says, "It's ashram's!"

Best thing so far is the pull-up bar. Why are adults in an orphanage? I smile at them, but I don't want to save the kids. Or the world. Pizza man feels the need to cut and run. Trying to remember how to cry. I wear a black t-shirt, while the Guru signs his emails "with light and love".

I've reached the furthest depths of homesickness—missing Allentown, PA. Not my family, not the people, not my work, but the big and growing grid of roads, TGI Friday's, Wawa ice cream, the prospect of roller coasters. Running laps around Trexler Park, mobility constrained by stoplights, tossing aside *The Morning Call* in favor of the *Wall Street Journal* unless there's an especially lurid headline. The not-really-winter winter, slush instead of snow, not wanting to watch as my paychecks go.

Ten times twenty makes twenty times ten,
I want to be upstate again.
Five times ten is ten times five,
let me deliver pizza pies.

Two times five is five times two,
thoughts, back up and let me through.
One times two is two times one,
is that a sinking or a rising sun?

Bean to the lima, lima to the bean,
dirty dogs worldwide come clean.
Goat to the goatherd, herd to the goat,
future and past, the mental moats.
All my life I've taken copious notes
which put half the holes in my holy boat.

Grime accumulates under my nails,
I collect the grime and put it for sale,
fingernail grime, fifty dollars a pail,
eat my grime like buttery snails.

I'd like to meet a cheetah
as she stalks knee-deep through
the Bhagavad Gita
munching Cheetos with her feet on the seat,
in too deep to see I'm
cheap, slow meat.

Lentils, lentils, where you going?
E-ZPass lane, stereo blowin'.
Lentils, lentils, yellow and tiny,
march like a middle school band behind me.
Lentils, lentils, can't you wait?
Pushing like a salesman, second date.
Lentils, lentils, not again—
your amendments always cost me friends.

Lentils and rice with a bit of spice
sounds nice, but you're rolling the dice,
flying a lightning kite
if you pick this mix
every single day—twice.

Beards are tradition,
mark a transition,
grab what you dish in
your hungry mouth,
pout with the lips,
leave necks eclipsed,
curl and billow and Brillo on south.
Catch pondering strokes
while protruding from cloaks,
are braided or dreaded or brushed or combed
and should come with a manual
or guarantee that sparrows won't take up a home.
Growing a beard's no effort at all
(except trimming the curtain's fall),
so let your follicles bring it—
evade the blade till your chin starts singing.

Dinner bell rings, kids appear.
Days stack into orphan years.

Ashram: Defragging the mind.

I lie in bed, draw my knees to my chest and try to breathe. And with every breath the past teases. The smell of the basement where I first played Nintendo. Picking out a mountain bike in Bedford Hills with my mother. Not at Caldor, at a real bike shop. I could have had almost any bike I wanted. And I chose a purple GT, not even considering whether I'd be teased for the color. Purple and black. Now with only a thin cotton comforter, the wooden bedboards pang my hip, shoulder, and ankle ball. I don't move. What else is there? The concrete floor? The bell rings for

lunch and again I don't move. Breathe. Just breathe. I've been at the
Ashram five days. To stretch my money. I have to change my ticket. I
have to return to the town of my birth and write for the local paper. Take
what cash I have left and go for it. Outside, across the garden, the
children's voices stack up as they pile in for the morning meal of rice and
not much more. The French couple in the room next door shuffles into
their sandals, grabs their aluminum plates, and bolts the door. Time to eat.
Buying tinfoil-wrapped weed in a Subaru's back seat behind D'Agostino's.
Coffee ice cream in Wolfeboro. The index card I taped next to my
bedroom's outlet as a message to my dad: Unplugging the stereo does not
save money. Skip this meal and no more food till tonight. I roll, drop my
legs off the edge of the bed, and sit up. One meal closer to home. Fine. I
slip into my sandals.

Everything: Accept it as if you chose it.

In the middle of the night: gotta piss. I swing my feet over the
edge of the bed. Into water? Fucking A, damn the builder, the monsoon,
and especially the Guru. I cross and find the light switch. The bedside rug
has partly damned the rain flowing in beneath the door. The water has
hooked a left and headed under the bed. A flood covers half the room,
roughly the shape of New York State. I wince, exhale. My neck is jacked.
Find the broom. Water an inch deep in the doorway, rain sprinkling
steadily on the porch, bubbles betraying the current into the room. For
the first time I notice the slant of the smooth floor. I slide across the
cement, round the corner, and get the hand broom. Squat and sweep (I've
learned something). Back in the room, I push a wave of water onto the
porch. It slides back. There's no drain out there. The porch wall has a
couple brick-sized holes, perfect drainage, but they sit atop a brick-high
bulkhead. Idiotic. I consider sweeping the water into the staircase, but no
one else is on this floor. They'll know I made the mess. I send a few
strokes under the door of the now-empty neighboring room. Grab the
bathroom bucket and sweep into it. I empty a few cupfuls into the shower

96

drain. Pointless. I pick my belongings off the floor, stack everything atop my one chair. Hit the light, return to the last dry spot of carpet, and wipe my feet. Shine a light beneath the bed to check the progress. The flood has narrowed to a tentacle. Watch a smudge on the dry zone disappear. Like seeing a boat on the horizon slide behind your thumb. With one knee up on the bed, I remember: gotta piss. I knead the torqued muscles of my neck and step back into the cold wet.

The Guru has a habit of addressing us from the balcony. He wears a gold sash. Who wears a gold sash? The children wear necklaces of the bald jowly strabismus-afflicted Mother. Their yellow bus proclaims above the windshield, "All Life is Life Divine."

In the morning, the Guru says, "My dear young man, how are you today?" This bastard knows full well I got flooded out last night. And has no idea about my jacked neck.

In the afternoon, the Guru calls my name. "This ice cream is for a birthday. My sister in America, she sent money so everyone could eat ice cream on her birthday. And you have come here from America. So you see everything is—" He spreads the fingers of each hand wide, then lattices them together. "The circle of ice cream," I say, contemplating the miracle of a nation of 300 million sending someone to a subcontinent of 1.1 billion from which it had received an immigrant.

After we eat, the Guru makes an announcement in Nepali.
I say, "What'd he say?"
"To take some ice cream to his mother."
"Where?"
A name I don't know. "I think 30 minutes, by car."
Delivery's nice, but the fuel costs—and the heat!

All Life is Life Divine on a yellow Swaraj Mazda bus. Bigger than a short bus, but no Furthur. Shatkona imposed on concentric circles for the bus's bindi, with Nepalese and Indian flags emerging from the top, crossed.

First, only his feet, swaying in the air, traversing the flat roof. His torso was hidden by a wall, a wall that failed to dispel the impression if he took one handstep too far, he'd topple over the edge. The next day, he poked his face from the bushes which screen his front door and we exchanged names. I provided my nationality; his was understood. And that evening—yesterday—he invited me for tea by calling from his balcony to mine. "But not after nine—" he said. "Seven?" "Yes, seven, seven is good." A minute later, in my room, my pen produced a strange note: TEA W/NEIGHBOR 7AM. BRING MANGO. The mango I'd been avoiding because I couldn't stomach the mess in my beard.

And now for tea. The neighbor says, "I get up at three every day and go for a wash." It's 7:15 a.m. and I'm sitting on a low stool, face to face with this man, Ram, face to peaceful face, a man who taught small children for twelve years in Upper Mustang, who then worked at the ashram for 14 years, who built a house with a room for his ancient mother. A man who has sent two apparently bright sons to school in the US (New York and Texas), who grows his own food organically, who has served me a light pink herbal tea in a tall glass, a man with athletic shoulders and waist, open listening eyes, and not a crease on his forehead. Face to face with the face I'm afraid I'll become. He's done the cooking, he tells me, because his wife is in bed with her period. He has a wife and he has a bed, but I can't picture him in the both at the same time. Men who give their lives to children. It makes me suspicious. The first thought, of course, is he might be a molester, which can't be investigated further at the moment (speaking of molesters, how about a single man who founds an orphanage?), and the second thought, the converse, is "He can't hang." This route he's taken, I'm nearly nauseated by its existence, its possibility as a valid option, at least on the personal level. It's right there, waiting at blahblahrecruiting.com, proclaimed as a Pretty Nice Life in the photo galleries of so-and-so ESL Café dot com. The teacher, his Thai wife, and their two fashionable children on vacation in Paris. They can afford to vacation in Paris.

Ram's food is exquisite. He asks if I know Angelica Kitchen in New York. Sounds New Yorky. The address? 300 E. 12th St. "Near Tompkins Square Park." Sure—I've traced the perimeter of the park, drunk, at every hour. Is this the place with the soul food spooned out heavy? The brunch spot we'd re-grease at? Or was that Life? He tells me I can stop by anytime. "No need to set a time, like in the West." "It'll be a surprise," I say. Meaning never. Once a week at best. This place is weirder than what I want to run from. Three pictures on the wall: A triptych of The Mother, bald head equally bald in all of them, jowls equally jowly, deified by self and others. My bowels have woken. Got to get out.

A person with a journal is a dangerous thing. In a pledge class, in the army, in jail. In an ashram. And that's not all the ashram shares with those three. A schedule to manage the group. An opacity to the outside world. A man in charge. And often, the bare minimum. The sanitary conditions of a fraternity, the personal time of the military, the home decor of prison. It's the ideal vacation spot for someone with two months of vacation and two weeks of funds.

The deuces come by surprise, any bite can be a depth charge or a time bomb that detonates a third of the way through meditation. Vegetarian food, the same formula every day—RICE, lentil or potato stew, wheat roti, a diabolical pickle (today was radish/mango), and after, homemade yogurt. I'm a man who likes to live dangerously. It slides out in a mustard yellow soft-serve, enough to supply a school bus with small cones. I can talk about it because everyone here shares details. Within our first five minutes of conversation, the Guru told me he'd had diarrhea the past two days. He is risen—at 4 a.m.! And when I inevitably get diarrhea from this earth-and-cow-stinking soapless kitchen, everyone's going to know.

Martin says to the Guru, "That was a beautiful talk you gave at meditation last night."

And the Guru says, "Were you at meditation last night?"

And I say, "No, ah, I didn't make it." Hesitation be damned, I looked him in the eye. He doesn't press the issue.

Martin turns his face to the sun of the Guru. "I'm going into the city today. I'll be back tomorrow." What will Martin do in the city? Pick up a Slim Jim of hash? No. Pick up a trek-hardened backpacker? Negative. Drop $15 on a full-service massage at one of Thamel's 150 or so parlours (yes, -*ours*)? Not a chance.

With Martin, it runs in the family. He met the Guru over dinner in Montreal at his mother's behest. "And once I met the guy..." he says, and you know what's coming. Convert, acolyte, disciple, and true believer. He spent four months here last year, and now he's back for his college's summer vacation. He's skinny, half Venezuelan (but of Spanish descent, he adds), likes baggy t-shirts and sweatpants with holes. "I had to come back, I mean, there's so much love—" Cut.

I say, "What's the story behind the earring?"

He says, "I got this here, last year. I wore it all the time in Montreal to remember the ashram. And I still have it."

It being a single dangly mobile of pink beads, with a silver tassel tail. Bold, but he pulls it off in a naive way. Kind of. He's a good guy. I mean, he smokes cigarettes. But I'm getting the feeling he would die for the cause. So when we smoke our nightly Shikhar, I can't confide in him. No matter, all I need is a notepad.

I sit on carpet in front of a Samsung flatscreen—how'd it get in here?—and watch the King of Nepal give a speech and leave the palace forever. I understand nothing except that babies with bells on their ankles are loud, and someone in the room is silently divesting themselves of the deadly.

Dark, dark night. I wake after an almost-wet dream involving the Lime Rock Park grandstand, a woman wearing glacier glasses, and a Leica. I grab a sock from the floor, stare into the sparkling Kathmandu valley, and jerk off. Recalling Valentine's Day, a week before I left home.

Embrace the moment, no guilt or anger. No past or future. And so despite Napoleon Hill's claims it'll sap my creative energy, I bust without remorse. Making progress.

The Guru explains the butterfly stretch: "You pull this part close to your anus."

I say, "Your heels?"

Rumor has it tonight's meditation will be followed by a movie. I might as well attend and toughen up my ankle bones. I'm the only one who doesn't genuflect to Sri Aurobindo and The Mother. Who wants to put their nose inches from this carpet? The children, the ground-down adults, the neighboring French couple (Sylvan has jack-in-the-box hair, Angelica's two front teeth are grey-blue), and Martin—they sing their way through hymns to the recently-deceased duo, and then the Guru appears in a grandpa sweater with the elbows worn through. He takes the smallest child in the room onto his lap and delivers slow motion kisses to each cheek. The child, big enough to walk and with a sunspotted look in its eyes, nearly disappears in the Guru's knobby hands. At the same time, Ganesh (teenager, not elephant god) enters with a DVD player under his arm. He hooks it to the TV in the corner, taking only a minute, and leaves a cable draped across the corner of the screen we're about to watch. It cuts a generous corner, but nobody complains. He fires up the DVD and someone hits the lights.

On screen: Camera, concept and editing by *somelongname@something.com.np*. Shameless. The video begins with a cut-per-second smorgasbord of ashram scenes. Cow udders, toes kicking soccer balls, uniformed students at desks, hand-to-mouth feeding, and so forth. Cut. Subtitle: *Transfer of Sri Aurobindo's Relics to Terai*. A wave of nausea passes over me, as it does whenever I hear someone clipping their nails. Relics. The Guru on screen carrying a tray of fruit with a box in the center, boarding a flower-draped Jeep, leading a costumed, singing procession through a standard-issue crowded street. The Guru standing before a sarcophagus of white marble, the crowd behind him. Subtitle: *The all-important moment of depositing the Relics.* The Guru putting the box in a slot with his clean right hand; the Guru as mason, troweling cement. Subtitle: *The celebration continues with dance.* Dancing and pit stains. Subtitle: *A most wonderful day indeed.* Sitting on the ground eating stew with the hands. Cut to an anxious white woman. Subtitle: *Tourist from Canada.* She regales the Guru. Three other Westerners: France, Australia, Canada; same deal. Cut to the Guru seated in front of the new, domed building's staircase, blotting out the sun, his eyes black pits. Not a hint of Abe Lincoln. The Guru says, "We are not a sect or religion, we are a way of life," and continues to deny classification for seven minutes. The whole thing stinks, and he who denied it supplied it. The video closes with the intro's same dizzying mashup, and the email address as the sole credit. Applause. Ganesh unhooks the DVD player. And the children yell, "One more time!" The Guru ribbons his hand through the air, *go on, go on...* I leave as Ganesh arranges a second screening.

Another morning. I shuffle into the dining room with my bowl and spoon, surrounded by incense production. Squat beside a scabby-necked kid. I say, "Professional incense factory." With all the activity, I'm not sure if the bell was for food, but I'm encouraged by the residue of milk in the bowl beside him. I walk to the door of the kitchen, where the steaming pot of milk sits on the floor. I squat again and offer my begging bowl. A breastfeeding woman ladles it half-full. "Black tea?" I ask, as I do each day. "No," she says. I left early last night, and that's why there's no tea. She doesn't want to go to the trouble. And why should she? I'm the guy who gets up late. Who hasn't lifted a shovel bigger than his spoon. I already know what she'll do at the next meal. She won't wash her left pointer, and when I arrive for my roti, she'll smear me into sick for a week. I know it.

The Guru: Skinny and tallish. His face tight and rubbery, his forehead bunched into infinite ripples, his eyes wide and near-wild, his nose probing, his mouth a jovial Jolly Roger with an gap between his two front teeth where the gums descend to a central fleshy stalagmite. His shoulders and frame—skeletal.

The kid says, "I think you should stay a long time."
Ouch. I don't even know this kid's name.

And Grandmaster Flash says, "There's a strike at the station." Specifically, at the Old Bus Park, Kathmandu. After a weekend in the city, there's no bus to Thankot, no microbus. It's a fuel price protest. Taxi— for 1500R? My negotiating power is nil. I can't start a bidding war, the base price holds at four digits. Can I walk? The map shows a road on the other side of the river bumping into the edge of the page with an arrow, the text above "Thankot"—the destination. A cop quotes it at two hours. The monsoon sky appears satiated for at least three. Option B, walk back to Thamel and pay for another night's room and dinner and breakfast and bus, plus innumerable willpower cave-ins, wagon falls, impulse satisfactions, and what-the-hells. Walking—it'll be like trekking, an adventure, and if the rain is too heavy I can find a room for cheap. It's good exercise, I've been wanting to do it anyway, I might catch a ride, and ultimately I go for it because it's what an Eagle Scout would do, regardless of his Puma sneakers and empty stomach and freeballing status in jeans.

The map from the tourism bureau is gold. Easy enough to follow, I take a route avoiding the square marked *Central Jail* and end up in capillaries, and wind in the general direction of the bridge. A bit of a rough neighborhood, but for every hotshot with forearm tattoos, there's a big tough mama leaning on a restaurant doorframe next to a pressure cooker. After the bridge it's the opposite, the road to Pokhara and the border is filled with arts and crafts trucks, painted and sculpted and arguing with musical horns. A standard subcontinental artery, lined on both sides with five-story buildings, and dark and dirty chutes into who-knows-where, and trash and shit, and people locked in open outcry trading. A never-ending uphill carnival midway, where you only can take in five percent of the stimuli on first pass, and what you catch swings from arousing to grotesque to absurd to mundane, and all the while you have to keep one eye on the ground to make sure you don't plant a foot in the nasty. The big chewed bones of something. A radiator replacement in progress. Now that's an ass. And of course, an actual ass tied to a doorway covered in what looks like dried cottage cheese, its eyes closed. Freddie Mercury speeds by on a motorbike and pops his eyebrows. *Hop on?* Pass a bus stand and you're the most popular in person in town. *Gora! Gora! Goragoragora!* I wrap a bandana around my mouth to fight a sudden rise in exhaust fumes, and a minute later see ALL LIFE IS LIFE DIVINE bombing down the hill. I flap my arms and jump, and the yellow bus pulls over fifty meters down the hill. I run and get in, and as the stranger at the wheel starts to drive, I ask him where he's headed. Terai? No thanks—I want to keep walking. He finds a wide spot and squeezes a U-turn. I urge him not to backtrack for me. Save the fuel, I'll walk. And then he pulls over at a mechanic's shop above where we met, and abandons ship.

A kid from the ashram gets on, maybe 16 years old, and says the man was the mechanic "making a trial". The kid plops into the driver's seat and I take the death seat, or shall we say the goodbye-legs seat in this flat-nosed clunker, and we're off again, ashram-bound.

I feel as cool as you can feel in shotgun, with my bandana around my neck, hat pulled low, radio loud, sitting sideways to give my legs a chance, elbow out the window. We pass a crowd of 300 people on the road, peering into something. The kid says a woman saw a statue in a dream, and took men to the spot, and they dug fifteen feet and found— Hanuman! And now everybody wants to see.

We pull off, pay a toll, get a ticket, and claw up a dirt road, the kid fighting through mud, stopping for chickens and goats (stalling twice on the restart—he's learning), cutting through a construction zone where a family is fighting, and finally parallel parking next to an eight-foot tall stack of bricks in the ashram driveway. Speaking as a driver, nicely done.

The Kathmandu businessman said, "If you sleep with a village woman, you'd better plan to marry her. Or else somebody's coming after you with a shovel."

Martin has diarrhea today, and in his weakness tells me he has a crush on Pavita. We debate whether the ashram follows Nepalese standards, is more conservative, or is a free-love commune. I suggest we ask the Guru what the sex rules are. Martin thinks anyone who has sex will be asked to leave—even Pavita.

I return to my room an hour later, and in the mirror there's a mess of white crust in my right eyebrow. Dandruff shampoo I forgot to rinse out. Smooth!

The intervals between meals are the exact amounts of time it takes to get hungry from the last meal.

Blind man taps down the mountain path, walking, no worries at all. Jesus, it takes balls to be blind in Nepal.

I'm washing my hands and the power goes out. It's good timing tonight. I'm done using the ashram's only computer, and twenty seconds ago I finished the post-computer dump. It would have been tricky in there. Back in my room, I find my headlamp on the bed, pull the candle plate to the center of the room, and kneel down to light them. The lighter wheel slips off its track—try, try again—broken for good. Damn. The power comes back on.

Now, when the power goes out, I don't immediately reach for my flashlight. I stand at the window as candles twinkle to life across the valley. Stars falling into a lake. The days are routine here at the ashram, though I've bent the routine knowing I won't be here long enough to benefit from ingratiation. I sleep through yoga at five and incense making at six, and I'm usually up for a bowl of hot milk at seven. Back to my room to read until nine, teach from ten until twelve, then crank out some pullups and bounce. I'm back for dinner.

The rain is starting. I'm going to be flooded again. Which is fine.

The Guru calls from his balcony to mine.

"Yes?"

"Come. Come here. Nepali sweets."

For once, I'm above him in altitude, but still I can't refuse. I've just had tea and a piece of gum, my only sugar of the day, and though the little bit was enough to make his offer seem like a chocolate bar on top of cake, I say, "Coming!" and fly down the stairs.

He meets me in front of his building and opens his bucket hand to reveal three brown globs. "Pustakari. Yesterday in Kathmandu I bought this Nepali sweet for everyone to have. You suck it, and then after a while, well..." He closes his hand and turns it upside down.

I cup my two together and receive the payload. "Thank you." I pop one in my mouth. "I like it. I mean, I've never tried it before. I mean, it's almost chocolatey..." His smiling silence always makes me babble, makes me feel like I'm babbling. "Thanks."

This place has multiple posters of Naughty Boy Krishna, on his knees under a cow with a teat in his mouth, the cow returning the favor by licking his ass. His mom Devaki in a sari with her own naughty smile, winding up to beat him with a stick.

Entering the hall for meditation during a power outage, I squeeze my way through a crowd of fifteen kids fanned around the Guru's door, gazing in at a single candle, above which the Guru sits on his bed, eating dal bhat. Is he speaking between bites? Or are they seeking illumination?

The house below my window has no windows and no door on its outhouse. In the mornings, their googly-eyed grandma squats over the hole. I'm amazed at her flexibility, and worry about the strain. Does she try to go only once a day? I don't enjoy watching. It's a foul, fragile sight.

A textbook found at the ashram says 700 men died in the American Civil War. The pink cast on the little girl's leg is starting to stink.

After meditation, I chase the Guru in the dark, calling his name. He keeps walking, head down, barefoot along the brick path. The moon lights his white kurta with the yellow scarf. Louder than I mean to, I call his name. "I have the key!" And then, "Samata said to give it back to you." Yes, I may be addicted to the internet.

"Yes, here. I can take the key." He turns back, I give it to him with two hands. "Your application has been submitted and now we are waiting to see if you are given a spot in the course." He's talking about the ten-day Vipassana retreat starting the first of July.

"Thank you." I hesitate to put my feet in the mud and cross pointy bricks to my sandals.

He says, "We are getting into the rainy season now, you know."

"It comes and goes."

"Like life. Yes." I'm sure he is smiling. He says, "Sometimes now it will rain for two, three days without break. This will be a canal, with all the water going down." Does he want a response? "But we are on the high ground. The water goes on past."

"I see."

"Have you been studying?"

"I've been doing a lot of reading." And not a lot of work to make this place work.

"Ah ha."

I use the silence to swivel my headlamp so I can look him in the eyes without blinding him, but the most I can manage is staring at his cheek, out here alone in the dark. "Well, I guess I'm going to go pass out. Goodnight."

"What time do you usually go to sleep?" This conversation is still going?

"I read for an hour or two, then go to bed. So maybe ten. Nine or ten. Alright, goodnight."

I descend the courtyard's stairs, down the hill toward the guest house. I hate having the last word with this guy. He doesn't give benedictions or dismissals, he leaves you to walk away as you hear his brain whirring behind you. On the topic of you. Or maybe he returns to a state of no thought, no processing, being at peace—I fear I'm describing enlightenment here—so quickly you want to assume he's still coupled to the prior exchange.

My sink doesn't work. My shower doesn't work. The toilet gets enough of a slow drip to flush once every two or three hours. Nobody believes me. They think I'm doing something wrong. I want to wash my hands and body, what with the kids picking lice out of each other's hair here, and a five year-old washing shit out of a toddler's shorts there. There—where we wash our dishes. When the water is fixed, and I rush out of my room and close the revived taps. I get an urge to finish the cookies. And guess who fixed it the water? Doesn't matter.

A girl who's a known lice carrier goes into the bathroom next to my room, and I want to yell *Hey! You still got the lice? Yeah? Then stay out of my bathroom!* But I don't.

The guesthouse speaks for the ashram. No windows on the massive valley-view side. You get a side-eye at best. The balconies face up the mountain, into the ashram. Which is also a damn fine view.

Heading to breakfast today, I run into an exodus from the dining room. Kids pouring out. Someone must have puked or shat themselves in there. Kapil says, "The girl inside, she is sick." I peek in to check out the splatterhouse, ready to hold my nose and get some food. In the middle of the room: A girl sprawled on her back, limbs out, eyes rolled white like she took a bullet. Jesus! Is she dead? Dying? She flaps an arm, mildly reassuring, and I join the scare-shortened food line.

Two girls fan the victim and talk in fast whispers. Maybe she fainted. I smell vomit. But what turns my stomach is that my instinct wasn't to help. I have a long way to go.